"Who'd have guessed it?"

Nina cuddled closer to John as she spoke. A smile softened her lips.

"Guessed what?" John looked into her eyes, and his brow creased in a frown that was here and gone.

"That slow, thoughtful John Sawyer was a crackerjack of unleashed virility in bed."

John's cheeks were already flushed, but Nina could have sworn that they grew more so. "I was inspired," he murmured.

"You certainly were." Her smile faded. She touched his face. "I didn't like you much when we first met. You were slowing me down."

"I still am. It's my cause."

"It won't work. I have to be at the office by 10:00 a.m. . . . unless you can convince me otherwise."

John kissed her gently, then less gently as his hunger grew. He rolled onto his back and pulled Nina on top of him. "Mmm . . ." Nina whispered. "Convince me more. . . ."

Dear Reader,

Welcome to Crosslyn Rise, a majestic estate on the North Shore of Massachusetts and the setting for Barbara Delinsky's long-awaited trilogy; three love stories that stand alone but together create a powerful saga of six lives linked by a common dream. The Crosslyn Rise trilogy appears in three consecutive months, beginning in October with *The Dream* and followed in November and December with *The Dream Unfolds* and *The Dream Comes True*.

Harlequin Temptation is proud to feature these dynamic, passionate romances from one of our finest authors, and we'd love to hear your comments. Please take the time to write to us.

The Editors
Harlequin Temptation
225 Duncan Mill Road
Don Mills, Ontario, Canada
M3B 3K9

CROSSLYN RISE

The Dream Comes True
BARBARA DELINSKY

Harlequin Books

TORONTO • NEW YORK • LONDON
AMSTERDAM • PARIS • SYDNEY • HAMBURG
STOCKHOLM • ATHENS • TOKYO • MILAN

Published December 1990

ISBN 0-373-25425-3

CROSSLYN RISE: THE DREAM COMES TRUE

1

EIGHT PEOPLE SAT around the large table in the board-room at Gordon Hale's bank. They comprised the Crosslyn Rise consortium, the men and women who were financing the conversion of Crosslyn Rise from an elegant, singly owned estate to an exclusive condominium community. Of the eight, seven seemed perfectly content with the way the early-morning meeting was going. Only Nina Stone was frustrated.

Nina hated meetings, particularly the kind where people sat at large tables and hashed things out ad nauseam. Discussion was part of the democratic process, she knew, and as a member of the consortium, with a goodly portion of her own savings at stake, she appreciated having a say in what was happening at Crosslyn Rise. So she had smilingly endured all of the meetings that had come in the months before. But this one was different. This discussion was right up her alley. She was the expert here. If her fellow investors weren't willing to take her professional advice now that the time had finally come for her to give it, she didn't know why in the world she was wasting her time.

Nina's business was real estate. She was the broker of record for Crosslyn Rise, the one who would be in charge of selling the units and finding tenants for the retail space. It was mid-May, nearly eight months since ground had been broken, and the project was finally ready to be marketed.

"I still think," she said for the third time in thirty minutes, "that pricing in the mid-fives is shooting low. Given location alone, we can ask six or seven. What other complex is forty minutes from Boston, tucked into trees and meadows, and opening onto the ocean? What other complex offers a health club, a catering service, meeting rooms and even guest rooms to rent out for visiting friends and relatives? What other complex offers both a marina and shops?"

"None," Carter Malloy conceded, "at least, not in this area." Carter was the architect for the project and the unofficial leader of the consortium. As of the previous fall, he was married to Jessica Crosslyn, who sat close by his side. Jessica's family had been the original owners of the Rise. "But the real estate market is lousy. The last thing we want is to overprice the units, then have them sit empty for years."

"They won't sit empty," Nina insisted. "Trust me. I know the market. They'll sell."

Jessica wasn't convinced. "Didn't you tell me that things weren't selling in the upper end of the market?"

"Uh-huh, but that was well over a year ago, when you were thinking of selling the Rise intact, to a single buyer. Selling something in the multiple millions was tough then. It's eased up, even more so in the range we're talking." She sent her most confident glance around the table. "As your broker, I'd recommend pricing from high sixes to mid sevens, depending on the size of the unit. Based on other sales I've made in the past few months, I'm sure we can get it."

"What kind of sales were those?" came the quiet voice of John Sawyer from the opposite end of the table.

Nina homed in on him as she'd been doing, it seemed, for a good part of the past hour. Of all those in the room, he disturbed her the most, and it wasn't his overgrown-schoolboy look—round wire-rimmed glasses, slightly shaggy brown hair, corduroy blazer with elbow patches and open-necked plaid shirt—that did it. It was the fact that he was sticking his nose in where it didn't belong. He was a bookseller, not a businessman. He knew nothing about real estate, and though she had to admit that he usually stayed in the background, he wasn't staying in the background today. In his annoyingly laid-back and contemplative way, he was questioning nearly everything she said.

"Three of those sales were in the eights, one in the nines, and another well over the million mark," she told him.

"For properties like ours?" he challenged softly.

She didn't blink. "No. The properties were very different, but the point is that, A, this community is in demand, and, B, there is money around to be spent."

"But by what kinds of people?" he countered in the slow way he had of speaking. "Of course, the superwealthy can spend it, but the superwealthy aren't the ones who'll be moving here. They won't want condo living when they can have ten-acre estates of their own. I thought we were aiming at the middle-aged adult whose children are newly grown and out of the house and who now wants something less demanding. That kind of person doesn't have seven or eight hundred thousand dollars to toss around. He's still feeling his way out from under college tuitions."

"That's one way of looking at it," Nina acknowledged. "Another way is that he now has money to spend that he hasn't had before, precisely because he no longer has those tuitions to shoulder. And he'll be willing to spend it. As he sees it, he's sacrificed a whole lot to raise his family. Now he's ready to do things for himself. That's why the concept of Crosslyn Rise is so perfect. It appeals to the person who is still totally functional, the person who is at the height of his career and isn't about to wait for retirement to pamper himself. He has the money. He'll spend it."

"What about the shopkeepers?" John asked.

"What about them?"

"They don't have it to spend. If you set the price of the condos so high, the rental space will have to be accordingly high, which will rule out the majority of the local merchants."

"Not necessarily."

"You'll give them special deals?"

"The rental space doesn't have to be that high."

"It can't be anywhere *near* that high—"

Her eyes flashed. "Or you won't move in?"

"I won't be *able* to move in," he said calmly.

With a glance at his watch, Gideon Lowe, the builder for the project, suddenly sat forward. "I don't know about you guys, but it's already nine. I'm losin' the best part of my day." He slanted a grin from Nina to John. "How about you two stay on here and bicker for a while, then give us a report on what you decide at the meeting next week?"

Nina didn't appreciate the suggestion, particularly since she suspected that Gideon's rush was more to see his wife than his men. She couldn't blame him, she supposed; he'd been married less than a month and was clearly in love. His wife, Christine, was doing the decorating for Crosslyn Rise. Nina liked her a lot.

Still, this was business. Nina didn't like the idea of staying on to bicker with John Sawyer when she wanted an immediate decision from the group. Keeping her voice as pleasant as possible, given the frustration she was feeling, she said, "I think this is something for the committee as a whole to decide. Mr. Sawyer is only one man—"

"One man," Carter interrupted, "who is probably in a better position than any of the rest of us to discuss the money issues you're talking about. He's our potential shopkeeper."

Jessica agreed. "Maybe Gideon is right. If the two of you toss ideas back and forth and come up with some kind of compromise before next week, you'll save us all some time. We're running a little short now. Carter has an appointment at nine-thirty in Boston, I have one in Cambridge." Murmurs of agreement came from around the table, along with the scuffing of chair legs on the highly polished oak floor.

"But I wanted to go to the printer with the brochure," Nina said, barely curbing her impatience as she stood along with the others. "I need the price information for that."

Carter snapped his briefcase shut. "We'll make the final decision next week." To John, he said, "You'll meet with Nina?"

Nina looked at John. The fact that he was still seated didn't surprise her at all. The consortium had met no less than a dozen times since its formation, and in all that time, not once had she seen him in a rush. He spoke slowly. He moved slowly. If she didn't know better, she'd have thought that he didn't have a thing in life to do but mosey along when the mood hit and water the geraniums in the window box outside the small Victorian that housed his bookstore.

But she did know better. She knew that John Sawyer ran that bookstore with the help of only one other person, a middle-aged woman named Minna Larken, who manned the till during the hours when John was with his son. Nina also knew that the boy was four, that he had severe sight and hearing problems and that her heart went out to both father and son. But that didn't make her any less impatient. She had work to do, a name to build and money to make, and John Sawyer's slow and easygoing manner made her itchy.

Typically, in response to Carter's query, John was a minute in answering. Finally he said, "I think we could find a time to meet."

Forcing a smile, Nina ruffled the back of her dark boy-short hair and said in a way that she hoped sounded sweet but apologetic, "Wow, this week is a tough one. I have showings one after another today and tomorrow, then a seminar Thursday through Sunday."

"That leaves Monday," Carter said buoyantly. "Monday's perfect." Putting an arm around Jessica's waist, he ushered her from the room.

"Carter?" Nina called, but he didn't answer. "Jessica?"

"I'll talk with you later," Jessica called over her shoulder, then was gone, as were all of the others except John. Feeling thwarted, Nina sent him a helpless look.

With measured movements, he sat back in his chair. "If it's any consolation, I don't like the idea of this any more than you do."

She didn't know whether to be insulted. "Why not?"

"Because you're always in a rush. You make me nervous."

She *was* insulted, which was why she set aside her normal tact and said, "Then we're even, because you're so slow, you make *me* nervous." But it looked as though the group would be expecting some sort of decision from John and her, and she couldn't afford to let them down. There were some important people among them. Impressing important people was one way to guarantee future work.

Hiking her bag from the floor to the table, she fished out her appointment book. "So, when will it be? Do you want to make it sometime next Monday, say late morning?"

John laced his fingers before him. "Next Monday is bad for me. I'll be in Boston all day."

"Okay." She flipped back a page, then several more. The seminar would be morning to night, and draining. No way could she handle a meeting with John on any of those days. "I could squeeze something in between three-thirty and four tomorrow afternoon."

He considered that, then shook his head. "I work then."

"So do I," she said quickly, "but the point is to fudge a little here and there." She ran a glossy fingernail down the page. "My last showing is at seven, but then I have a meeting—" She cut herself off, mumbled, "Forget that," and turned back one more page. "How about later today?"

When he didn't answer, she looked up. Only then did he ask, "How much later?"

She studied her book. "I have appointments through seven. We could meet after that."

He freed one of his hands to rub the side of his nose, under his glasses. When the glasses had stopped bobbing and his fingers were laced again, he said, "No good. I'm with my son then."

"What time does he go to bed?"

"Seven-thirty, eight."

"We could meet then. Can you get a sitter?"

"I can, but I won't. I have work to do in the store."

"But if you don't have a sitter—"

"I live on the second floor of the house. If I'm downstairs in the store and he cries, I can hear it."

She sighed. "Okay. What time will you finish your work?" It occurred to her that she would rather meet with John later that day, even if it meant cutting into the precious little time she had to herself, than having the meeting hanging over her head all week.

"Nine or ten."

"We could meet then. I'll come over."

He eyed her warily. "Isn't that a little late for a meeting?"

"Not if there's no other time, and it looks like there isn't."

His wariness persisted. "Don't you ever stop?"

"Sure. When I go to bed, which is usually sometime around one or two in the morning. So—" she wanted to get it settled and leave "—are we on for nine, or would you rather make it ten?"

"And you work all day long?"

"Seven days a week," she said with pride, because pride was what she felt. Of six brokers in her office, her sales figures had been the highest for three years running. Granted, she didn't have a husband or children to slow her down, but the fact remained that she worked hard.

"When do you relax?"

"I don't need to relax."

"Everyone needs to relax."

"Not me. I get pleasure in working." She held her pen poised over the appointment book. "Nine, or ten?"

He studied her in silence for a minute. "Nine. Any later and I won't be thinking straight. Unlike you, I'm human."

His voice was as unruffled as ever. She searched his face for derision, but given the distance down the table and the fact of the glasses shielding his eyes, she came up short. "I'm human," she said quietly, if a bit defensively. "I just like to make the most of every minute." By way of punctuation, she snapped the appointment book shut, returned it to her bag and hung the bag on her shoulder. "I'll see you at nine," she said on her way out the door.

There was no sound behind her, but then, she hadn't expected there would be. John Sawyer would have needed at least thirty seconds to muster a response, but she'd been gone in fifteen. By the time the next fifteen had passed, her thoughts were three miles down the road in her office.

WITHIN FIFTEEN MINUTES, after stops at the post office and the dry cleaner, she was there herself. Crown Realty occupied the bottom floor of a small office building on the edge of town. The brainchild of Martin Crown, the firm was an independent one. It had the advantage over some of the larger franchises in its ties to the community; the Crown family had been on the North Shore for generations. Over and above two local restaurants and a shopping mall, the family assets included the weekly newspaper that made its way as far as Boston. In that weekly newspaper were real estate ads that would have cost an arm and a leg elsewhere. The money saved was tallied into profits, and profits were what interested Nina Stone the most.

Nina had plans for the future. She was going to have her own firm, have her own staff, have money in the bank, stability and security. She'd known this for ten years, the first four of which she'd spent in New York. Four years had taught her that as tough as she was, New York was tougher. So she'd moved to the North Shore of Massachusetts, where the living was easier and the market was hot. For six years, she'd doggedly worked her way up in the world of real estate. Now the end was in sight. With one more year like the ones behind her and a respectable return on her investment in Crosslyn Rise, she'd have enough money to go out on her own.

Having a solid name, a successful business and scads of money meant independence, and independence meant the world to Nina.

"Hi, Chrissie," she called with a smile as she strode through the reception area. "Any calls?"

"Pink slips are on your desk," was the receptionist's reply.

Depositing her bag, Nina snatched them up, glanced through even as she rearranged them in order of importance, then settled into her chair and reached for the phone. The first and most urgent call was from a lawyer whose client was to pass papers on a piece of property that morning. At his request, the meeting was put off for an hour, which meant that Nina had to shift two other appointments. Then she returned calls to a seller with a decision on pricing, an accountant trying to negotiate his way into prime business space and a potential buyer who had heard a rumor that the price of the house she was waiting for was about to drop.

Nina was on the phone chasing down that rumor when a young woman appeared at her door. Lee Stockland, with her frizzy brown hair, her conservative skirts, blouses and single strand of pearls, and the ten extra pounds she'd been trying to lose forever, was a colleague. She was also a good friend, one of the best Nina had. Their personalities complemented each other.

Nina waved her in, then held up a finger and spoke into the phone.

"Charlie Dunn, please."

"I'm sorry, Mr. Dunn's not in the office."

"This is Nina Stone at Crown Realty. It's urgent that I speak with him." She glanced at her watch. "I'll be here for another forty-five minutes. If he comes in during that time, would you have him call me?"

"Certainly."

"Thanks." She hung up and turned to Lee. "Maisie Stewart heard that 23 Hammond dropped to eight-fifty." She swiveled in her chair. "It wasn't in the computer last night. Have you seen anything today?"

"Nope."

Nina brought up the proper screen, punched in the listing she wanted and saw that Lee was right. She sat back in her chair. "If word of mouth beat this computer, I'll be furious. Charlie knows the rules. Any change is supposed to be entered here."

"Charlie isn't exactly a computer person."

Nina tossed a glance skyward. "Do tell. He claims you can't teach an old dog new tricks, but I don't agree with that for a minute. What you make up your mind to do, you do." With barely a breath, she said, "So, what did the Millers think of the house?"

Lee took the chair by Nina's desk. "They weren't thrilled to see me rather than you, but I think they liked it. Especially her, and that's what counts."

Nina nodded. "I know him. He'll see every little flaw and be tallying up how much it will cost to fix each one. Then he'll balance the amount against the price of the house and go back and forth, back and forth until someone else's bid is accepted and it's too late. Then we'll start right back at the beginning again." She sighed, suddenly sheepish, and fiddled with her earring. "Thanks, Lee. Jason is a pain in the butt. I really appreciate your taking them out."

"You appreciate it?" Lee laughed. "I'm the one who appreciates it. If it weren't for the clients you give me, I'd be twiddling my thumbs all day."

Nina couldn't argue with that. As brokers went, Lee was an able technician. Given a client, she did fine. But she didn't know the meaning of the word 'hustle,' and hustling was the name of the game. Nina hustled. When she wasn't showing a potential buyer a piece of property, she was meeting with a seller, or phoning potential others with offers of appraisals, or organizing mailings to keep her name and her business in the forefront of the community's mind.

Lee didn't have the drive for that, and while once upon a time Nina had scolded her friend, she didn't any longer. Lee was perfectly happy to work less, to earn less, in essence to serve as Nina's assistant, and Nina was grateful for the help. "You're a lifesaver," she said. "The Millers insisted on going early this morning. I couldn't be two places at once."

"Speaking of which," she gave a pointed look at Nina's bright red linen dress, "I take it that's your power outfit. How did it go at the bank?"

Nina's mouth drew down at the corners. "Don't ask."

"Not good?"

"Slow. Sl-ow." She began to pull folders from her bag. "Let me tell you, working with so many people is a real hassle. To get one decision made is a major ordeal."

"Did they like the brochure?"

"I think so, but I never got a final judgment on it, because they got hung up discussing the pricing of the units."

"What did they decide on that?"

Nina's phone buzzed. *"Nothing,"* she cried, letting her frustration show. "They want me to meet with this one guy—" She picked up the phone. "Nina Stone."

"Ms. Stone, my name is Carl Anderson. I was given your name by Peter Serretti, who worked with you on your new computer system."

Nina remembered Peter clearly. He had indeed worked with her, far more closely than she had wanted. Long after she learned to operate the system, she'd been plagued by phone calls from Peter asking her out. So now his friend was calling. She was immediately on her guard.

"Of course, I remember Mr. Serretti. What can I do for you, Mr. Anderson?"

"I'm actually calling from New York. My wife and I are both in education. We'll be moving to Boston in August. We were thinking of buying something on the North Shore. Pete said you were the one to talk with."

Nina felt an immediate lightening of her mood. "I'm sure I am," she said with a smile for Lee, who had settled into her chair to wait. "What kind of place are you looking for?"

"A condo. Two to three bedrooms. We have no children, but have a dog and two cars."

Nina was making notes. "Price range?"

"Two-fifty, three hundred tops." He rushed on apologetically. "We just can't handle anything more than that. When we visited Pete, we were impressed with the North Shore. If I'm totally out of my league, tell me."

"You're not, not at all." Crosslyn Rise was out of the question, both in terms of price and availability, but there were other options. "There's an older three-bedroom condo on the market for two-ninety-five, and several more updated two-bedrooms in the same range. But there's a new complex that you should probably see. It's in Salem, near the harbor, and it's beautiful. About half of the units have been sold, but there are still some wonderful three-bedroom ones that would fall within your range." She described the units, at times reading directly from the promotional packet that Lee had smoothly slipped her.

Carl seemed pleased. "We thought we'd drive up Friday and spend Saturday and Sunday looking. Would that be all right?"

"Uh, unfortunately, I'll be at a seminar all weekend—" her eyes met Lee's "—but one of my associates could certainly show you as much as you'd like to see." She frowned when, with a helpless look, Lee gave a quick shake of her head.

"Pete recommended you," Carl insisted. "He said you knew what you were talking about. I had an awful time with a broker here when we bought the place we're in now. She messed up the Purchase and Sales agreement, and we nearly lost the place."

Nina loved hearing stories like that. "I don't mess up Purchase and Sales agreements."

"That's what Pete said."

"Is this weekend the only time you can come?"

"This is the only weekend my wife and I are both free."

"Then let me suggest this. I'll go through all the listings, come up with everything I think might be worth seeing, and my associate will do the showing." Lee was still looking helpless. "You and I can talk first thing Monday morning when I'm back in the office. I'll be able to handle things from there."

Carl Anderson seemed satisfied with that. After taking note of his address and phone number, plus additional information regarding what he wanted, Nina hung up the phone. Her eyes quickly met Lee's. "Problem?"

"I can't work this weekend," Lee said timidly.

"Oh, Lee. You said you could. I've been counting on you to cover for me while I'm away."

"I can for Thursday and Friday, but—" she hesitated for a split second before blurting out "—Tom wants to go to the Vineyard. I've never been to the Vineyard. He's already made reservations for the ferry and the hotel, and he's talking about lying on the beach and browsing through the shops and eating at terrific restaurants—" She caught her breath and let out a soft, "How could I say no?"

Nina felt a surge of frustration that had nothing to do with work. "You can't. You never can, to Tom. But it's always last minute to a dinner or a movie or a weekend away. Why doesn't he call sooner?"

"He just doesn't plan his life that way. He likes spontaneity."

"Baloney. He just can't make any kind of commitment. He goes here, goes there, calls you when he gets the urge. He uses you, Lee."

"But I like him."

"You're too good for him."

"I'm not," Lee said flatly. "I'm twenty-eight, and I've never been married. I'm not cute like you, or petite, or blue eyed. I can't wear clothes like you do or polish my nails like you do. I'm not aggressive, and I'll never earn much money, so I'm not much of a bargain. But Tom is good to me."

Nina died a little inside. Each time she heard a woman use those words, no matter how innocent they were, she thought of her mother. So many times Maria Stone had said the same—*but he's good to me*—and for all the men who'd been "good" to her, she had ended up with nothing. Nina ached at the thought of that happening again, particularly to someone she cared about, like Lee.

Coming forward on the desk, she said with force, "You're not a lost cause, Lee. You're attractive and smart and warm. You're the one who taught me how to cook, and arrange flowers, and save bundles by shopping in the stores *you* found. You have lots to offer a man, lots more than me. You don't need to stoop to the level of a Tom Brody. If you want male company, there are plenty of other men around."

"Fine for you to say. You attract them like flies, then you swat them away."

"I do not."

"You're not interested in a relationship."

"I'm not interested in marriage, and I'm not interested in being kept, but I date. If an interesting guy comes along and asks me to dinner, I go."

"When you have time."

"Is there anything wrong with that?" Nina asked more gently. They'd had the discussion before. "Work means a lot to me. It's my future. At this point in my life, the investment I make in it means a whole lot more than the investment I might make in a man." Under her breath, she muttered, "Heaven only knows the return stands to be better."

Lee heard the low muttering and sighed. "Speak for yourself. Those of us who aren't so independent are looking all over for Mr. Right, but I think all the Mr. Rights are taken."

"Just wait. Give all those Mr. Rights a chance to divorce their first wives, then they'll be yours for the taking. I'm told they're far better husbands the second time around."

"I want Tom first. I think I have a chance with him, Nina. I really do."

But Nina knew more about Tom Brody than she let on. She had seen him in action against her boss years before, when he'd tried to renege on an agreement that was signed and sealed. "He's not right for you, Lee. He's a huckster with his eye out for the fast lane. When he hooks onto it, he'll be long gone. What you need is someone softer, slower, less driven." The image that popped unbidden into her mind made her snort. "You need a guy like John Sawyer."

"Who's John Sawyer?"

"A member of my consortium. He's invested in the Rise, but he's not a businessman, at least, not in the strictest sense of the word. He sells books. He's a thinker."

Lee arched an interested brow. "Married?"

"His wife died. He has a little boy who's four."

Lee's interest waned. "Oh. I'm no good with kids. I don't think I want to get into that. Forget John Sawyer."

Nina's thoughts flipped back to the meeting earlier that morning, then ahead to the one to come later that night. "I wish I could. The man might prove to be the biggest thorn in my side since Throckmorton Malone." Throckmorton Malone was a perennial house-shopper. He found a house he liked, put down a deposit, started bickering with either the builder or the owner or the owner's agent about the smallest, most insignificant details, then pulled out of the deal after handfuls of others who might have been interested had been turned away.

"No one could be that big a thorn."

Nina sighed. "Maybe. Still, this one could give me gray hair. He thinks we're pricing the units too high. He thinks he knows the market. Worst of all, the rest of the group thinks he knows what he's talking about, so they're making me meet separately with him to try to come to some sort of compromise."

"That's not so bad. You can convince him to see things your way."

"Yeah, but he's so—" she made a face as she searched for the word, finally exploding into a scornful "—*blah*. He's so calm and casual and unhurried about everything. He has all the time in the world to mull over every little thing. What ought to take five minutes will take fifty with him. Just looking at him frustrates me."

Lee showed a hint of renewed interest. "He's good-looking?"

"Not to *my* way of thinking. He's too bookish. I mean, we're talking thin and pale. Drab. Boring."

"Is he tall?"

Nina had to think about that, then think some more. "I don't know. I don't think so. Funny, I've never really noticed. He's that kind of guy, blink and you miss him." She frowned. "Mostly when I see him he's sitting down. Everyone else get up to leave, he stays in his seat. He doesn't move quickly. Ever." She sighed. "And I have to meet with him at nine o'clock tonight. Who knows how long he'll drag out the meeting." She grimaced. "Could be he'll put me to sleep."

"That'd be novel." They both knew Nina rarely slept. She had too much energy to slow down for long.

With a glance at her watch, Nina was out of her chair. "I'm meeting with the Selwyns at the Traynor cape in five minutes. Gotta run."

"About this weekend—" Lee began.

"Not to worry," Nina assured her. Taking a file from the corner of the desk, she slipped it into her bag. "I'll get someone else to cover."

"I'm really sorry. I hate letting you down."

Turning to her, Nina said in earnest, "You're not letting me down, at least not about filling in here. You have a right to a life, and if you haven't been to the Vineyard, you *have* to go. I just wish you weren't going with Tom."

"I'll be fine. Really."

"Famous last words," Nina said softly, gave Lee a last pleading look, then murmured, "Gotta run."

2

NINA'S DAY WAS BUSY ENOUGH to prevent her from giving the impending meeting with John much thought until she returned to her office at seven, with all other appointments behind her and two hours to fill before nine. Filling them wasn't the problem. She had more than enough paperwork to do, and if she finished that, there were phone calls to make. But the urgency wasn't the same as it would have been at the height of the workday. So her mind wandered.

She thought about Crosslyn Rise, and how pretty the first of the units, nestled in among trees at the duck pond, were beginning to look. She thought about the brochure she had so painstakingly put together with the artist who'd drawn pictures of the Rise, and the printer, and the fact that she felt it should already be in circulation. She thought about the pricing, the arguments both ways, her own conviction and John's. She thought about his slow, slow way of thinking and talking and her own preference for working more quickly. The more she thought about those things, the more frustrated she grew. By the time she finally got into her car and drove to The Leaf Turner, she was spoiling for a fight.

The house stood close to the center of town and was a small white Victorian, set in relief against the night by the glow of a street lamp that stood nearby. The second floor was dark, the first floor lit. Walking to the front door as though it were the middle of the day and she were out shopping for a book, she turned the brass knob and let herself in.

"Hello?" she called, closing the door behind her. When there was no response, she called again, in a more commanding tone this time, "Hello?"

"Be right there," came a distant voice, followed after a time by the leisurely pad of rubber-soled shoes on the back stairs, which was followed, in turn, by John's appearance. At least, it was the appearance of someone she assumed to be John. His face was partially hidden behind the carton he was carrying, a carton that looked to be heavy from the way he carefully lowered it to the ground. When he straightened, he looked her in the eye and said in that slow, quiet way of his, "You're right on time."

For a minute, she didn't speak. The man who had emerged from behind the carton had John's voice and features, but that was the extent of the similarity to the man with whom she served on the Crosslyn Rise consortium. This John's face wasn't pale, but flushed with activity and shadowed with a distinct end-of-the-day beard. This John's face slightly shaggy brown hair was clustered into spikes on his forehead, which glistened with sweat. As she watched, he mopped a trickle of that sweat from his temple, displaying a forearm that was leanly muscular and spattered with hair.

"I aim to please," she said lightly, but she couldn't take her eyes from him.

This time he ran the back of his hand over his upper lip. "I'm short of space up here, so the courier service puts deliveries in the basement. I've been carting books around, trying to get things organized. If I'd realized I was going to build up a sweat, I'd have showered and changed."

"No problem." She was still wearing the red dress she'd had on since dawn. "It's the end of the day. Besides," she added in an attempt to set the tone for their meeting, "we won't be long enough to make it worth the effort. I'm sure we can hash out our differences in no time."

He responded to the suggestion with a nonchalant twitch of his lips. "I don't know about that, but you're welcome to try." Leaning over, he slit the carton open with a single-edged blade, set the blade back on the counter and pulled the flaps up. "Go ahead. I'm listening."

He was wearing the same plaid shirt he'd been wearing that morning, only he'd paired it with jeans. They fit his lean hips so familiarly that his shoulders looked broad. She hadn't expected that. She had thought he'd be spindly under his corduroy blazer. She had also thought he'd be weak, but from the looks of the carton he'd been carrying—and the fact that, though sweaty, he wasn't winded in the least—she'd been wrong. She could see strength in his forearms, in his shoulders, in the denim-sheathed legs that straddled the box as he began to unload it.

Straightening with an armful of books, he looked at her. "I'm listening," he said again, and the mild derision in his eyes wasn't to be mistaken. Only when she saw it, though, did she realize something else.

"You're not wearing your glasses." She'd never seen him without them before, had simply assumed they were a constant.

"They get in the way sometimes."

"Don't you need them to see?"

"When I'm reading. Or driving. Or thinking of doing either." Turning away, he hunkered down by a low riser near the cash register and began to stack the books, turning one right, then one left, alternating until his arms were empty. When he was finished and stood, she realized yet another thing. Though he wasn't tall by the standards of men like Carter Malloy and Gideon Lowe, in relation to her own five foot two, he was long. She guessed him to be just shy of six feet.

"Something wrong?" he asked with maddening calm.

She felt a warm flush creep up from her neck, all the more disconcerting because she wasn't normally one to blush. Rarely did things take her by surprise the way John Sawyer's physical presence had. "No, no. It's just that you look so different. I'm not sure that if I'd walked in here cold, I'd have connected you with the man at the bank."

He considered that for a minute, then shrugged. "Different circumstances. That's all. I'm still the same guy you're gonna have to give a slew of damn good reasons to before I'll agree that those condominiums should be priced out of sight."

His words stiffened her spine, counteracting any softening she'd felt. "Out of sight? A million dollars would be out of sight. Not six hundred thousand."

"You were arguing for six-fifty to seven-fifty."

"The local market supports that."

He held her gaze without a blink. "Are there any other condominiums—not single-family homes, but condominiums—selling in that range around here?"

She didn't have to check her listings. At any given time, she knew the market like the back of her hand. "No, but only because there haven't been any built that would qualify. Crosslyn Rise does. It's spectacular."

He rubbed the bridge of his nose. "Is that reason to price it so high that no one will be able to enjoy it?"

"Plenty of people will be able to enjoy it."

"Not at that price, and if the condos don't sell, you can kiss the shops goodbye. No merchant—least of all me—wants to open up in a ghost town."

"It wouldn't be a ghost town," Nina scoffed, but softly. He'd raised a good point, namely the connection between sales of the condos and success in renting out the shops. Granted, the shops would hardly be relying on the residents alone; none would survive without the patronage of the public, for which purpose public access had been carefully planned. But the public wouldn't be coming to shop if the rest of the place looked deserted.

Returning to his carton, John bent over and filled his arms a second time with books.

Helpless to look away, Nina noticed the way his dark hair fell across his neck, the way the plaid shirt—darkened in random dots of sweat—stretched across his back, the way his fingers closed around book after book. Those fingers were long and blunt tipped. Rather than being delicate, as she'd have assumed a bookworm's to be, they looked as sturdy as the rest of him. She had the sudden impression that his laid-back manner hid a forbidding toughness. If so, she could be in for trouble.

Wanting to avoid that, she gave a little. "Okay. We could set a limit at seven. The smaller units could be in the low sixes, the larger ones closer to six-ninety-five."

John gathered books into his arms until he couldn't hold any more, then moved to the riser and arranged a second pile beside the first.

"John?"

"You're still a hundred grand too high. There's no need to price gouge."

"There's need to make a profit. That's the name of the game."

"Maybe your game," he said complacently, and returned for a third load.

"And not yours? I don't believe that for a minute. You put your own good money into the consortium, and from what I hear, there isn't a whole lot more where that came from."

One book was stacked on another. He neither broke the rhythm nor looked up from his work.

"The only reason," she said slowly, hoping that maybe a man who spoke slowly needed to hear slowly in order to comprehend, "why a man stakes the bulk of his savings on a single project is if he feels he has a solid chance of getting a good return."

John straightened with the last of the books. "Exactly."

She waited for him to go on. When he simply turned and began arranging a third pile by the first two, she moved closer. "The higher we price these units, the greater your return will be. The difference of a hundred-thousand over two dozen condos is two-and-a-half million dollars. That spells a substantial increase in our profit." She frowned. "My Lord, how many of those books do you have?"

"Twenty-five."

"And you really think you'll sell twenty-five at $22.95 a pop? I could believe five, maybe ten or twelve in a community this size. But twenty-five? How can you be so optimistic about books and so pessimistic about condos?"

Taking his time, he finished stacking the books. When he was done, he stood, wiped his palms on his thighs and gave her a patronizing look. "I can be lavish with books because the publishers make it well worth my while. When they're trying to push something, they offer generous deals and incentives. They're pushing this book like there's no tomorrow."

"It stinks."

He shrugged. "Sorry, but that's the way the publishing world works."

"Not the deals. The book. It stinks."

"You've read it?"

For the first time, she had caught him off guard, if the surprised arch of one brow meant something. "Yes, I've read it."

"When? I thought you worked all the time."

"I never said that."

"Sure sounded it from the way you were standing at the bank this morning struggling to squeeze in a single meeting with me."

"This week's worse than most because of the seminar. It's four intensive days—"

"Of what?"

"Classes on commercial real estate transactions. In the past year or two, I've been doing more with stores and office buildings. I've been wanting to take this seminar for six months, but this is the first time it's been offered at a time and place I could handle."

He gave her a long look. "Funny, I assumed you could handle most anything."

"I can," she said without flinching. "But it's a matter of priorities. Let me rephrase what I said. This is the first time the seminar's been offered at a time and place that work into my schedule without totally screwing up everything else."

He gave that brief thought. "So, when do you read?"

"At night. Late."

"When you can't sleep because you've got yourself wound up about everything you should be doing but can't because no one else is awake to do it with you?"

She was about to summarily deny the suggestion when she realized how right he was. Not that she intended to tell him that. "When I can't sleep, it's because I'm not tired."

The look in his eye was doubtful, but he let her claim ride. "And you didn't like this book?"

"I thought it was self-indulgent. Just because an author writes one book that wins the Pulitzer Prize doesn't mean that everything else that author writes is gold, but you'd have thought that from the hype the book was given. So I blame the author for her arrogance and the publisher for his cowardice."

"Cowardice?"

"In not standing up to the author and sending her back to rewrite it. The book *stinks*."

John pondered that. After a minute, he said, "It'll make the bestselling lists."

"Probably."

"And I won't lose a cent."

Given deals and incentives and bestselling status, he was probably right, she mused.

"Out of curiosity, if nothing else," he went on leisurely, "people will buy the book. No one will be broken by $22.95. Readers may be angry, like you are. They may feel gypped. They may even tell their friends not to buy the book, and I may, indeed, have two of these stacks standing here three months from today, just as they are now. But one disappointing book won't hurt my business." His eyes took on a meaningful cast. "At Crosslyn Rise, on the other hand, a thirty-three percent sell rate will hurt and hurt bad."

Nina shook her head. "The analogy's no good. You're comparing apples and oranges—sweet apples and moldy oranges, at that. Crosslyn Rise is quality. This book isn't. No one who buys into the Rise will ever say that it wasn't worth the money. In fact, some of the sales will probably come about by word of mouth, people who buy and are so excited that they spread the excitement."

"People who are stretched tight financially may not be able to feel much excitement."

"People who are stretched tight financially have no business even looking at the Rise, much less buying into it."

John's eyes hardened. "You're tough."

"I'm realistic. The Rise isn't for first-time home owners. It isn't for twenty-five-year-olds who've just gotten married and have twenty thousand to put down on a mortgage that they'll then pay off each month by painstakingly pooling their salaries." She held up a hand, lest he think her a snob. "Listen, I have properties that are less expensive, and I have clients who are looking for that. But those clients aren't looking for Crosslyn Rise, or if they are, they should be awakened to the rude realities of life."

"Which are?"

"Everything costs. *Everything.* If you don't have money in your pocket to pay for what you want or think you need, the cost comes out of your hide and is ten times more painful."

Her words hung in the air. Even more, her tone. It was hard and angry, everything Nina was accused of being from time to time by one detractor or another whose path she crossed. Now she held her breath, waiting for John Sawyer to accuse her of the same.

He didn't say a word. Instead, after studying her for what seemed an infinite stretch, he turned away, bent and swept up the empty carton, and forcibly collapsed it as he walked from the room.

She waited for him to return. Gnawing on her lower lip, she kept her eyes on the door through which he'd gone. His footsteps told her that he'd taken a flight of stairs, leading her to guess he'd returned to the basement, but all was still. She shifted her bag from the left shoulder to the right, shifted her weight from the right foot to the left, finally glanced at her watch. It was after nine-thirty, getting later and later, and they hadn't reached any sort of agreement on Crosslyn Rise.

"John?" she called. When the only thing to greet her was silence, she let out a frustrated sigh. Wasted time drove her nuts, and this meeting spelled wasted time in capital letters. She and John Sawyer had some very basic differences. He was relaxed and easygoing, she was driven. Neither of them was going to change—not that change was called for. All that was called for was some sort of compromise recommendation for the pricing of the units at Crosslyn Rise.

At the sound of a quiet creaking over her head, she looked up. He must have gone upstairs, she realized, probably to check on his son, and she couldn't begrudge him that. It would have been nice if he'd said something, formally excused himself, told her he'd be back shortly, rather than just walking out. She hadn't associated relaxed and easygoing with rude before, nor had she associated rude with John. Slow, mulish, even naive, perhaps. But not rude.

He didn't like her. That explained it, she guessed. The hardness that came to his eyes from time to time when he looked at her spoke clearly of disapproval, which was all the more reason why she should finish her business and leave. She wasn't a glutton for punishment. If he didn't like her, fine. All they needed was to come up with a simple decision, and she'd be gone.

The creaking came again from upstairs, this time more steadily. Soon after, she heard footsteps on the back stairs, but they went on longer than they should have. It didn't take a genius to figure out that he'd gone on down to the basement, and in the wake of that realization, she realized something else. She didn't like John Sawyer any more than he liked her.

Annoyed, she stalked toward the back room, turned a corner until she saw the stairs and called out an impatient, "I haven't got much time, John. Do you think you could come up here and talk this out with me?"

"Be right up," he called nonchalantly. She could well have been the cleaning lady, for all the attention he was giving her.

Spinning on her heel, she returned to the main room of the shop, where, for the first time, she took a good look around. The bookstore took up the entire front portion of the house. Working around tall windows, a fireplace that looked frequently used, a sofa and several large wing chairs, bookshelves meandered through what had once been a living room, parlor and dining room. The overall space wasn't huge, as stores went, but what it lacked in size, it made up for in coziness.

Antsy, Nina began to prowl. Passing a section of reference books, she wandered past one of history books, another of fiction classics, another of humor. As she wandered, her pace slowed. That always happened to her in bookstores and libraries. Whether she intended to or not, she relaxed. Books pacified her. They were nonjudgmental, nondemanding. They could be picked up or put down with no strings attached, and they were always there.

At the shelves holding recent biographies, she stopped, lifted one, read the inside of its jacket. She liked biographies, as was evidenced by the pile of them on her night shelf, waiting to be read. Tempted by this one but knowing that she didn't dare buy another until she'd made some headway with the pile, she replaced the book and moved toward the front of the store. At the cookbooks, she stopped. One, standing face front, caught her eye, a collection of recipes put together by a local women's group. She took it from the shelf and began to thumb through.

"Don't tell me you cook."

Nina's head flew up to find John's expression as wry as his voice, but neither of those things held her attention for long. What struck her most was the surprise she felt—again—at the way he looked. Tall, strong, strangely masculine. She hadn't expected any of those things, much less her awareness of them. The relaxation she'd felt moments before vanished. "Yes, I cook."

He turned to put down another carton where the first had been. Looking back at her, his eyes were shuttered. "You work, you read, you cook. Any other surprises?"

At least they were even, she mused. He surprised her in not being a total wimp, she surprised him in being a businesswoman who cooked. She still didn't understand his dislike for her, but there was no point in pursuing it. Their personal feelings for each other didn't matter. If Crosslyn Rise was the only thing they had in common, so be it.

"It's getting late," she said with studied patience as she watched him bend in half and slash the new carton open. "Do you think you could take a break from that for a few minutes so that we can settle the matter of pricing?"

Straightening slowly, he slipped the blade back onto the counter. In measured cadence, he said, "I've been listening to everything you've said. You're not swaying me."

"Maybe you're not listening with an open mind."

He gave the possibility consideration before claiming, "My mind is always open."

"Okay," she said in an upbeat, "why don't you run *your* arguments by me again?"

He arched a casual brow. "Would it do any good?"

"It might."

After studying her for several long moments, he bent to open the box and began to unload books.

"John," she protested.

"I'm getting my thoughts in order. Give me a minute."

Tempering her impatience, she gave him that. During its course, he carried half a dozen books to one shelf, half a dozen to another. She was beginning to wonder whether he was deliberately dragging out the time, when he came to face her. His skin wore the remnants of a moist sheen, but his eyes were clear.

"I believe," he said slowly and quietly, "that we should keep the pricing down on those units because, one—" he held up a long, straight finger "—we stand a good chance of selling out that way, which in turn will make the shops more appealing both to shopkeepers and to the general public—" he held up a second finger, "two, we'd attract a better balance of buyers, and three, the profit will be more than respectable." He dropped his hand and turned back to the box of books.

"Is that it?"

"That's enough." Hunkering down, he started to fill his arms. "Didn't I win you over?"

"Not quite."

With a sidelong glance, he shot back her own words. "Maybe you're not listening with an open mind."

"I always have an open mind."

"If that were true, you'd have already given in. My arguments make sense."

"Mine are stronger."

"Yours have to do with profit, and profit alone."

She wanted to pull her hair out. "But profit is what this project is *about*!"

"Right, and you could blow it all by getting greedy. The entire project will be jeopardized if we overprice the goods."

"Okay," she said with a sigh, "if the units aren't snapped up in six months or so, we can reduce the price."

He shook his head. "That smacks of defeat, and it'll taint the whole thing. The longer those units sit empty, the worse it'll be." He sighed patiently. "Look, the duck pond will be completed six months before the pine grove, and the meadow six months after that. If we don't sell the duck pond first thing, there's no way the pine grove will sell, and if the pine grove doesn't sell, forget the meadow."

"Okay," Nina said, trying her absolute best to be reasonable, "how about this. How about we price the duck pond in the sixes, then move up into the sevens as we move toward the meadow."

"How about we price the duck pond in the fives, then move up into the sixes as we move toward the meadow." He reached for more books.

Bowing her head, she squeezed her eyes shut and pressed two fingers to her brow. "This isn't going to work."

"It'd work just fine if you'd listen to reason."

Her head came up, eyes open and beseeching. "But I'm the *expert* here. Pricing property is what I do for a living! If I was off the wall, I wouldn't be as successful as I am!"

Arms filled with books, John straightened and gave her a look that was shockingly intense. "You're successful because you push with such force and persistence that you wear people down. But you're barking up the wrong tree when it comes to me. I'm not the type to be worn down."

Nina stared up at him, stunned by the vehemence of his attack and its personal nature. She couldn't believe what she'd heard, couldn't believe the anger that had come from the quiet, contemplative, laid-back bookseller. Swallowing something strangely akin to hurt, she said, "Why do you dislike me? Have I done something to offend you?"

"Your whole *manner* offends me."

"Because I work hard and earn good money? Because I know what I want and fight for it? Or because I'm a woman?" She took a step back. "That's it, isn't it? I'm a strong woman, and you feel threatened."

"I'm not—"

"Don't feel singled out or anything," she said quickly, and held up a hand. "You're not alone. I threaten lots of men. I make them feel like they're not fast enough or smart enough or insightful enough. They want to put me in my place, but they can't."

John's look was disparaging. "I wouldn't presume to know where your place is, and I doubt you do, either. You want to wear the pants in the family, but you're so busy trying to get them to fit that you blow the family part. How old are you?"

"It doesn't matter."

"It does. You should be home having babies."

She stared at him in disbelief, opened her mouth, closed it again. Finally she sputtered out, "Who are you to tell me something like that? You don't know anything about me. You have no idea what makes me tick. And even if you did, these are the 1990s. Women don't stay home and have babies—."

"Some do."

"And some work. It's a personal choice, one for *me* to make."

"Clearly you have."

"Clearly, and if you were any kind of a man, you'd respect that choice." She was suddenly feeling tired. Hitching her bag to the other shoulder, she headed for the door. "I think we've reached a stalemate here. I'll call Carter tomorrow and let him know. There's no way you and I can work together. No way."

"Chicken."

She stopped in her tracks, then turned. "No. I'm being practical. My standing here arguing with you is an exercise in futility. My arguments won't change your mind, any more than yours will change mind. We're deadlocked. So we'll have to do what I wanted to do from the start, let the whole committee hear the arguments and take a vote. And we'll chalk up this time to—to—client development."

"What does that mean?"

"That some day when you're selling this house and you want the bitchiest broker to get the most money for you, you'll give me a call." With that, she tugged open the door and swept out into the night. She was down the wood steps and well along the front walk before she heard her name called.

"Nina?"

"Save it for the bank," she called back without turning, raised a hand in a wave of dismissal and rounded her car.

"Wait, Nina."

She looked up to find John eyeing her over the top of the car.

"Maybe we should try again," he said.

"It'd be a waste of time." Opening the door, she slid behind the wheel.

He leaned down to talk through the open window. "Why don't you give me some time to think."

With one hand on the wheel and one on the ignition, she said, "Buddy, you could think till the cows come home and you wouldn't see things my way."

"Maybe we could meet halfway, you'd come down a little, I'd come up."

That was the only thing that made any sense, she knew, but the idea of meeting John Sawyer again didn't appeal to her in the least. "Why don't you suggest that next Tuesday at the meeting?"

"They're expecting a recommendation from us."

"We can recommend that the consortium take a vote." She started the car.

"Look," he said, raising his voice so that its even timbre carried over the hum of the engine. "It doesn't matter so much to me if they think we couldn't come to some kind of consensus. Hell, I'm just a bookseller who's trying to make a little money by investing in real estate on the side. But you're supposed to be the master of the hard sell. I'd think you'd want to impress those guys at that table in any way you can."

She did. No doubt about it. Staring out the front window into the darkness with both hands on the wheel, she said, "If we can agree right now to go with figures halfway between what you want and what I want, we've got our consensus."

"I think we ought to discuss it."

"That's the only solution."

"I still think we ought to discuss it."

Earlier, she had thought him mulish. She thought it again now. John had to be one of the most stubborn men she had met in years. Turning her head only enough to meet his gaze, she said, "That sounds just fine, only there's one small problem. We went through the whole week this morning, and the only time we both had free was tonight. Now tonight's gone. So what do you suggest?"

"We find another time."

She shook her head. "Bad week."

"Then the weekend."

"I told you. I have a seminar. It runs from nine to five every day, and I'll have to allow an hour before and after for travel."

"So you'll be home by six. We can meet then."

Again she shook her head. "I'm moving a week from Monday. Every night after the seminar is reserved for packing. I have to get it done."

"I'll help you pack."

Like hell he would. Eyes forward, she set her chin. "No."

"Why not?"

"Because I can do it myself."

"Of course you can," he said indulgently. "But I can help. I'm not the scrawny weakling you imagined I'd be."

Her eyes shot to his. "I never said—"

"But you thought. So you were wrong. And I can help you pack."

"You can *not*. I don't want your help. I don't *need* your help."

He was silent then, his expression a mystery in the dark. Finally, sounding even-tempered and calm, the John she'd known from the bank, he said, "Tuesday morning before the meeting. I'll meet you at Easy Over at seven-thirty. We'll talk over breakfast." Before she could say a word, he gave the side of the car a tap and was off.

"John!" she called after him, but she might just as well have saved her breath. He didn't move quickly, but he moved smoothly, covering the distance to the house and disappearing inside without a glance behind.

3

NINA PREPARED CAREFULLY for breakfast Tuesday morning. After wading through her wardrobe and discarding anything red, purple or lime green, she chose a beige suit that was as reserved as anything she owned. That wasn't to call it conservative. The blazer was nipped in at the waist over a skirt that was short and scalloped, exposing a whisper of thigh with every move. In an attempt to tone that down, she left the matching, low-cut gauzy blouse in her closet in favor of a higher necked silk. With a single strand of pearls around her neck and pearl studs at her ears, she felt she looked as traditional as it was possible for Nina Stone to look.

Her goal was to impress John Sawyer—not in any sort of romantic way, because she *certainly* didn't think of John that way, but in a business way. Normally she dressed in the bright, chic, slightly funky style that had become her trademark; clients came to her because they saw someone who was one step ahead of the eight ball. Somehow she didn't think that was where John Sawyer wanted to be, but she wanted him to be on her side when it came to marketing Crosslyn Rise, so it behooved her to impress him.

She arrived at Easy Over, a light-breakfast and lunch place not far from the bank, at seven-thirty on the dot. When she saw no sign of John, she took a table, ordered a pot of coffee and waited. He arrived five minutes later, wearing loose khaki pants, another plaid shirt, a slouchy brown blazer and glasses. Looking slightly sleepy, he slid into a chair.

"Sorry," he murmured. "Had a little trouble getting out." His eyes fastened on the coffeepot. "Is that fresh?"

She nodded, lifted the pot and filled the cup waiting by his place. "Anything serious?"

"Nah." He took a sip of coffee, then a second before setting down the cup, sitting back in his chair and catching her eye. "That's better. I didn't have time for any at home."

"What happened?"

He took another drink, a more leisurely one this time as though he were just then settling in to being his normal slow self. "My son isn't wild about the sitter. He didn't want me to leave."

"I thought kids nowadays were used to sitters. Don't you have one every day?"

"He likes the afternoon ones. They're high school girls with lots of energy and enthusiasm. For morning meetings at the bank, I have to use someone else. She's kind enough, and responsible, but she doesn't relate so well with him."

"He must be very attached to you."

"I'm all he has."

Nina thought about the boy's mother, wondered how she had died and whether the child remembered her. She wasn't about to ask John any of those things, though. They weren't her business.

"What'll it be, folks?" the waitress asked, flipping the paper on her pad and readying a pen.

Nina didn't have to look at the menu. She'd been at Easy Over enough to know what was good. "I'll have Ronnie's Special. Make the eggs soft-boiled, the bacon crisp and the wheat toast dry. And I'll have a large TJ with that." She watched the waitress note everything, then turned expectant eyes toward John.

He hadn't opened the menu either, but he seemed thoughtful for a minute. "Make that two," he paused, "only I want my eggs scrambled, my sausages moist and my rye toast with butter."

"Juice?" the waitress prompted.

"OJ. Large." Still writing, the waitress ambled off. John turned placid eyes on Nina. "For a little girl, you eat a whole lotta food."

"I have to. I rarely make it to lunch, and dinner won't be until eight or nine tonight."

"That's not healthy."

She shrugged. "Can't be helped. I'm into my busiest season. If I don't make the most of it, it'll be gone, and then where will I be?" With the reminder, she pulled up the folder that had been waiting against the leg of her chair, set it down in front of her and opened it up. "I spent awhile yesterday working with figures." She lifted the first sheet from the folder, but before she could pass it to him, he held up a hand.

"Not yet."

"Not yet?"

"Not before breakfast." He settled more comfortably in his seat. "I can't deal with business before breakfast."

"But this is a *business* breakfast. That means we eat while we talk."

His gaze touched the clean white Formica surface before him. "We haven't got any food yet. Let's wait on business."

Nina wanted to say that if they did that, they would not only be wasting good time, but if she had to go past

Plan A to Plan B or C, they might well run *out* of time before they reached an agreement. She wanted to say that first thing in the morning was the *best* time to discuss business, while they were the freshest. She wanted to say that they were due at the bank at eight-thirty, which, given John's tardiness and the time they'd already spent in chitchat and ordering, left them not much more than forty-five minutes.

She didn't say any of those things, because John's eye stopped her. She saw something in them, something strong enough to penetrate his glasses, something with a quiet but forceful command. She also saw that his eyes were amber, then looked more carefully and didn't see it at all. She remembered it. It must have registered on her subconscious the last time she'd seen him.

Carefully, with her heart beating a hair faster than it had been moments before, she set down the paper, sat back in her chair, crossed her hands in her lap and wondered what they would talk about in the time before their food arrived. There were a million things she could ask him, things she was curious about, like his wife and his son and his interest in books. Only none of that was her business.

She was used to talking. She *always* talked. Her role in life was to keep things moving, to win people over, to make sales. But she didn't know what to say to John.

She was beginning to feel awkward—and annoyed at that—when he asked, "Did you get your packing done?"

Relieved, she nodded. "Most of it."

"I trust you had other people to help you."

"No."

He arched a questioning brow and shook his head. She shook her head right back.

"No stream of admirers dying to show off their muscles?"

His tone was deferential, his expression benign. Still she had the feeling that somewhere inside he harbored a grudge. "No stream of admirers. No men at all. Why would you think that there were?"

"You're an attractive woman. You must have men all over you."

"I'm an *independent* woman. I couldn't bear to have men all over me. I told you I didn't need anyone's help."

"You told me you didn't need *my* help."

"Then you took it too personally. I didn't—don't— need anyone's help. When I do, I hire it and pay for it. By check," she tacked on, just so he didn't think she was trading her body for something. Men tended to think that way, and she hated it. The few men—precious few men—she'd been with in her thirty-one years had known that she gave because she felt affection and attraction, and because she knew they wouldn't demand anything more. They never did. She was as free as a bird, and glad of it.

"Where are you moving to?"

"Sycamore Street."

His brow flickered into a frown. "I go down Sycamore all the time. I don't remember seeing any For Sale signs—or were you able to get an inside scoop and snatch something up before it hit the open market?"

There it was again, the deferential tone, the benign look, the little dig underneath. Looking him straight in those amber eyes of his, she said, "I'm not buying. I'm renting the second floor of a duplex, and, yes, I snatched it up before it hit the market. That's one of the perks of being a broker, and it's perfectly legal."

She had been direct enough to issue a challenge and expected him to meet it. Instead, he simply looked surprised. "You're renting? I'd have thought a successful woman like you would be living in a spectacular house on a spectacular piece of land with a spectacular view of the ocean."

"I'm not that successful. Not yet." But she intended to be. One day, she'd have enough money to buy anything her heart desired. "Where I live right now isn't as important as saving as much money as I can."

"You put a whole lot into Crosslyn Rise."

"No more than you." They'd each seen the figures.

"That's a whole lot."

She thought about the sum. "Uh-huh."

"And you want to open your own business."

Her brow went up. "Who told you that?"

"Carter," he answered factually. "When the consortium was forming. Just like he told you about me. So when do you think you'll do it?"

"I don't know. It depends on how much money we make on Crosslyn Rise and how soon." Her hand went to the first paper on her pile, but before she could address herself to its contents, the waitress placed a large glass of tomato juice in front of her. She smiled her thanks and opened her mouth to speak to John when he stopped her with a hand.

"Not yet. I need food first."

"There's food," she said, pointing to his orange juice. "Drink up, then I'll talk."

Rather than taking a drink of the orange juice, though, he drained the last of his coffee and refilled the cup. "Aren't you happy at Crown?"

After a moment's consideration, she gave a one-shouldered shrug. "As happy as I'd be working for someone else, but I've always wanted to be on my own."

"Independent."

"That's right."

"So you can rake in the most bucks?"

She raised her chin. "It's not as much the money as the freedom. I don't like having to answer to someone else."

"Marty Crown's a nice guy."

"A very nice guy. I could have done a lot worse picking a boss." Not that she'd left that to chance. Before moving up from New York she had researched each and every real estate agency in the North Shore area. She'd picked Crown for its reputation, its connections and Martin.

"Does he know your plans?"

"No, and I'd rather he not," she advised, sending John a look that said she was trusting him to keep her secret. "I've done well for Martin in the six years I've been here. He's made good money from my sales, and I don't begrudge that. It's the way things work. He gets his share in exchange for giving me a forum to work and to learn. I'm a much better broker now than I was when I came. Whether I have Martin to thank for that, or myself, isn't important. What's important is that if I can take out of Crosslyn Rise double what I put in, I'll be in great shape to make my move." Feeling that to be as smooth a segue as any, she once again fingered the top sheet in her file.

Once again John stalled her. "That's a lot of money," he said with thought-filled preponderance. "I'd have thought you could pretty much set up a real estate brokerage wherever you wanted with little more than a telephone."

"Not the kind of brokerage I want," she said, and let her dreams momentarily surface. "I want something classy. I want to either buy a house and do it over, or rent the best commercial space available. Then I want to decorate with the best furnishings, the best window treatments, the best artwork. I want a secretary, a sophisticated telephone system to make certain parts of my work easier, a computer setup to handle the latest programs and handle them well. I want to design a distinctive logo and stationery, and I want to advertise." She took a breath. "All of that costs money."

"I'll say," John said, and sat quietly back, studying her as though she were something foreign that he couldn't quite understand. "Couldn't you start small? Do you need everything all at once?"

"Yes. That's the whole point. Real estate agencies are a dime a dozen around here. Granted, some are better than others, and those stand out. But for a new one to spring up and attract enough of a clientele to be successful, drastic measures are called for. From the very first, my agency has to be different. It has to attract attention. I think I can do it if, A, my offices are elegant, B, my staff is courteous, hardworking and smart, and, C, I advertise like hell."

"Your staff?"

She sent him a dry look. "I'm not doing all the work on my own. That would be suicide. The whole point is to have people who are answerable to me, to teach them and train them, let them do their work, then take *my* cut in the profits. Isn't that the way successful entrepreneurs do it?"

John didn't answer. He took a slow drink of his juice, set it down, then pushed his utensils out of the way when the waitress delivered plates filled with eggs, meat and toast.

Mindful that once they had food in their stomachs, John would be willing to talk business, Nina began to eat. She cracked her eggs, scooped them from the shell onto the wheat toast, gave them a light sprinkling of salt.

John's fork seemed stuck in the first of his scrambled eggs. "I'm surprised," he said unhurriedly, "that you want to set up business around here. If the goal is to make money and buy your freedom—"

"Not buy. Ensure."

"Ensure. If that's what you want, wouldn't you be better in a large place where, by virtue of sheer numbers of people, the market would be more active?"

"I've been there. I didn't like it."

"Why not?"

"Too impersonal. I may be hard, driven, aggressive, ambitious, even ruthless—people have called me all those things—but I like being able to greet the local grocer by name and have him greet me the same way. Besides," she added with a glance out the window, "I do love the ocean."

John followed her gaze briefly before returning to her. "When do you have time to see it?"

"I see it. Here and there. Coming and going." She nudged her chin toward his plate. "Eat up. Time's passing."

"Ever spend a day at the beach?"

"A day? No. An hour or two, maybe. Any more and I get itchy."

"You never wanted just to lie out on the sand for hours listening to the sound of people and the surf?"

"No. There's too much to do."

He took a bite of his eggs, then swallowed. "That's sad."

"Maybe for you. Not for me. I'd much rather get brief glimpses of the ocean lots of different times in the course of a day, know that it's there, even listen to it at night at the same time that I'm getting something else useful done, than sit doing nothing on the sand."

He looked baffled. "But don't you ever just want to go out and enjoy it for itself, rather than as an accompaniment to something else?"

"Why should I? It's the best accompaniment in the world. It makes anything else I'm doing that much nicer."

"That's sad," he said again, and Nina found herself getting irked.

"I don't see *you* with a tan."

"I haven't had time yet this spring. But I will. You can count on it. As soon as lessons let up a little for my son, we'll be hitting the beach."

Nina was about to ask what lessons he meant, when she caught herself. The child had a handicap. She didn't want to put John on the spot. Besides, his personal life wasn't her affair.

With a tolerant shrug, she said, "Different strokes for different folks. What works for you doesn't necessarily work for me, and vice versa. It's no big thing, John. Really." He didn't believe her, but that wasn't her worry. Crosslyn Rise was. "Listen, I'd really like to get to those papers." She glanced at her watch. "We have to be at the bank in less than half an hour."

"How was your seminar?"

"My seminar was fine." She put her hand on the top paper. "What I have here is my personal recommendation. I've broken the project down by size and expected date of completion—"

"Did you learn a lot? At the seminar."

She paused, stared, nodded. Then she patted the paper. "The more I thought about it over the weekend, the more I realized that we hit on something good last time we talked. The idea of—"

"Was it worth the four days?"

She took a breath for patience. "I'd say so."

"You're a better broker for it?"

"I'm more knowledgeable." She took another breath. "The idea of pricing the units progressively—"

"Don't you ever get tired?"

She pressed her lips together. "Of work? I told you. I love my work."

"But don't you ever get *tired*?"

"You mean physically fatigued?"

"Mentally fatigued. Don't you ever want to stop, even for a little while?"

"If I do that, it'll take me longer to reach my goal."

"What about burnout?"

"What about it?"

"Doesn't it scare you?"

"Not particularly. If I get where I'm going, I'll have plenty of time to take it easy, without the risks."

"What are the risks?"

"Of taking it easy now?" She didn't have to take time to think. She lived with certain fears day in, day out. "Loss of sales. Loss of reputation. Loss of status in the agency. There are other brokers out there just dying for my listings. If I'm not around, if I'm not working, if I'm not on top of things, if I'm not getting results, I lose."

In a rare instance of expressiveness, his mouth twisted in disgust. "I get tired just listening to you."

"Then don't," she snapped. "Don't ask me questions, and you won't have to listen to my answers. All I want—" she slapped the paper beside her plate "—is to come to some sort of decision here!"

John stared at her. She glared back. Gradually his stare softened into study, and before she knew it, she felt the same kind of quiet force emanating from him that she'd felt before. As had happened then, her heartbeat picked up, all the more so when his amber eyes began a slow, almost tactile meandering over her face. She felt their touch on her cheeks, her nose, her chin, then her mouth, where they lingered for a while to trace the bow curve of her lips.

The indignation she felt moments earlier was forgotten, pushed from mind by a strange, all-over tingle. "John?" Her voice wobbled. She cleared her throat. "I, uh, really think we should talk."

He wasn't done, though. His gaze dropped to her throat, touching the smooth skin there before slipping down over silk to the gentle swell of her breasts.

Even sitting, she felt weak in the knees, which made so little sense at all that a flare of pique shot through her. "*John.*"

His eyes rose. "Hmm?"

"I *need* to show you my *papers.*"

"What papers?"

She rapped the folder. "*These.*"

He looked at the folder, then looked back at her. Along the way, his mouth hardened. "You won't let it go, will you?"

"Let it go? But this is why we met!"

He said nothing, just stared at her. Not even his glasses diffused the strength of that stare.

She felt penetrated. "Wasn't it?"

Slowly he shook his head.

"Then why?"

"To have breakfast."

"You insisted on this meeting just for *breakfast*?"

Slowly he nodded.

"But *why*? You could have had breakfast for less money and with less hassle if you'd stayed home with your son. Why on *earth* did you drag me out here if you didn't have any intention of discussing Crosslyn Rise?"

"We'll discuss Crosslyn Rise. When we're done eating."

"So what do I do until then?" she asked in exasperation.

"You slow down. You take a deep breath. You look out that window and watch the sea gulls. You have a second cup of coffee and take the time to smell the brew." His voice lowered, growing sharper and more direct. "You're rushing your way through life, Nina. If you're not careful, the whole thing will be over and you won't know what in the hell you've missed."

Incredulity holding her mute, Nina stared. She had to take a deep, deep breath and give a solid swallow before she was able to say, "Last time I looked, this was my life. Seems to me I should be able to do what I want, and if that means rushing, I'll rush."

His voice came out gentler than before, but no less direct. "Not with me, you won't."

She sat back in her chair. "Fine." Two could play the game. She hadn't wanted this breakfast, anyway. All along, she had wanted the committee to take its vote. "Fortunately, I won't *be* with you beyond this meeting." She smiled. "Take your time. Eat. I'll just sit here and enjoy the scenery."

SHE WORKED HARD at doing that. After an eternity, with barely ten minutes until they were due at the bank, John invited her to show him the papers she'd brought. Staying calm, patient and professional, she went through them. With surprising ease, they came to an agreement on the third of her plans. Together they walked to the bank.

Sixty minutes later, when Nina returned to her office, she was like a steam kettle ready to blow. Slapping the folder sharply on her desk, she squeezed her eyes shut, put her head back and let out an eloquent growl. Its sound brought Lee in from next door.

"How'd it go?"

"Don't ask."

"Which plan did he go for?"

"C, damn it."

"And the consortium agreed?"

Nina nodded. Seconds later, she threw a hand in the air. "Don't ask me why I didn't argue more. I should have."

"Plan C is just fine."

"It's not aggressive enough."

"So why *didn't* you argue more?"

"Because—because—" she struggle for the words, finally blurting out, "because John Sawyer wore me down, that's why."

"I thought he was *blah*."

"He is."

"But he wore you down." Lee grinned in a curious kind of way. "That's a change. Usually it's the other way around. You must be losing your touch." When Nina gave her a dirty look, she said in an attempt to appease, "Sometimes the most blah people can be forceful, just because they take you by surprise."

But it wasn't that, Nina knew. It was John's persistence, his molasses-slow approach and a doggedness that was built of reason. His will was stronger than she'd expected, and, as fate would have it, his will coincided with that of the majority of the consortium.

Not for the first time, Nina vowed that she would never again involve herself in a project where decisions were made by committee. Unfortunately, she was stuck with this one to the end. "Crosslyn Rise may be the death of me yet." Snatching up the pink slips that were waiting, she flipped sightlessly through, then flattened them back on the desk. "The *worst* of it is that they want me to keep working with him. Can you believe that? They see him as kind of a lay advisor. So even though consortium meetings won't be held more than once a month through the summer, they're expecting John and I to meet once a week."

"That shouldn't be too hard."

"It's a royal waste of time, a total frustration." She sent a beseeching look skyward. "Someone up there better help me out, or I'll be a raving lunatic by the time summer's done." Eyes dropping back to the desk, she sighed. "At least I can give the printer the go-ahead to print those brochures." Moving the folder aside, she drew up a pad of paper. At the top, she wrote Call Printer. "I want to have an introductory Open House over the Fourth of July weekend, something with lots of hoopla to launch the selling campaign." To the list, she added, Call Christine, then Call Newspaper. Her pen went back to the Christine part. "*If* the model apartment is ready. Chris was aiming for the first of the month. It'll be impressive." Looking at Lee, she asked, "Have you been up there lately?"

Lee shook her head. "I'm waiting for you. Maybe today, after lunch?"

Something about the way Lee mentioned lunch gave Nina pause. She dropped her eyes to her desk calendar. Catching in a breath, she said, "Lunch! That's right!" She had forgotten all about it. With a grin, she looked up. "Happy birthday, Lee."

Lee blushed. "Thanks."

"I'm sorry. Wow, I should have been thinking about that when you first walked in here, but I've been so annoyed all morning. Hey, how does it feel to be twenty-nine?"

"You've been there. How did it feel to you?"

"I don't know. It came and went so fast, I think I missed it." For a split second, she remembered what John Sawyer had said, then pushed her mind on to more meaningful things. "So, we'll go out for lunch to celebrate. Any other plans?"

"I'm meeting my parents in town for dinner."

"Nice," Nina said with enthusiasm, though she couldn't help but wonder about Tom Brody. If there was something real going on between Tom and Lee, he should have been the one to take her to dinner on her birthday.

As though reading her mind, Lee said, "Tom and I celebrated last night." She touched her earlobe. "See?"

Nina was a stickler for her own appearance, dressing for the part she wanted to play. She carefully shopped for clothes and accessories, and wore them unselfconsciously once they were hers. There, though, her interest in fashion ended. She was far more apt to notice the overall effect of a person's clothing than the details of it. That was why she hadn't noticed Lee's earrings before.

Looking back, she didn't know how she'd missed them. They lit up Lee's ears in a way that neither gold, silver nor neon enamel could. "Wow," she breathed, coming out of her chair for a closer look. "Those are *gorgeous*."

"They're three-quarters of a karat each. Tom said to make sure I insured them."

Nina wanted to say that if Tom Brody had style, he'd have given her a year's worth of insurance along with the gift. But Tom had flash, not style. There was a difference.

"Definitely insure them," Nina said. She didn't add that that way Lee would be sure to have something of value when Tom left her behind. Nina wasn't a spoiler. But she felt awful. "It's too bad he can't join you tonight. Has he ever met your parents?"

"No. He has to be in Buffalo. It's just as well," Lee reasoned indulgently. "My parents would be looking Tom over as husband material, and that kind of pressure is the last thing Tom needs. He has enough pressure with work."

Nina felt momentarily chilled. Making excuses for a man was a sure sign that a woman was giving more than she was getting. But before she could say that, Lee made for the door.

"Martin is having a root canal. I told him I'd cover for him. He has some people coming in from the Berkshires. Their daughter is starting at Salem State in the fall and they want to buy a condo for the four years she's here."

Nina was hearing that same story more and more often. She supposed that if she had kids she'd want to do the same thing, since, given rents versus tax benefits and property appreciation, it made sense. Of course, she didn't have kids, so it was a moot point.

"How about I make reservations for twelve-thirty?" she asked.

"Sounds great," Lee said. "I'll be back here by twelve. See you then."

Nina waved a goodbye, then looked again at her desk calendar. The fact that she'd forgotten about lunch was nothing new. At the end of a given day, when she looked over her program for the next one, business appointments were the things she saw. Fortunately, she didn't have anything that would conflict with Lee's birthday celebration. She liked Lee a lot. She felt good about taking her out.

She was also grateful for the opportunity to eat, since she hadn't had much of the breakfast she had so glibly ordered at Easy Over. John had distracted her. Even when he'd been leisurely eating his own food, she hadn't eaten much. He made her stomach jump.

Annoyance, she told herself. Annoyance and irritation. John was the kind who, in his innocent way, gave people ulcers.

Actually, it was a wonder he was so calm, given the problem he had with his son. It couldn't be easy for him raising a child alone. She wondered about the extent of the boy's problems, wondered what kind of schooling those problems entailed. She wondered whether John ever got frantic, threw his hands into the air and gave up. Some parents did that when confronted with a frightening situation. Her mother had, more than once.

Something nagged in the back of her mind. Lifting the collection of pink slips that she'd barely seen earlier, she set one after another aside until she came to the one that had caused the nagging. It was a message from Anthony Kimball, the medical director of the Omaha nursing home where her mother lived. The call had come in promptly at nine that morning. The message requested a callback.

Lifting the phone, Nina punched out the number that she knew by heart. "Dr. Kimball, please," she asked. She gave her name, then waited while the call was transferred.

"Nina?"

"Yes, Dr. Kimball. I got your message. Is something wrong?" It wasn't often that Anthony Kimball called her, and when he did, there was usually a problem.

"I'm not quite sure. Your mother had some sort of seizure during the night. Her blood pressure fell dangerously low. We have her stabilized now, and there doesn't seem to be any other side effect from whatever the seizure was, but I thought you ought to know. This may be the start of the weakening that we've been expecting."

Nina swiveled her chair away from the door and bowed her head. "Is she comfortable?" she asked quietly.

"As far as we can tell."

"Is she aware of anything?"

There was a pause, then a quiet, "I don't believe so."

Nina sighed. "I guess we should be grateful for that." She pressed a hand to her eyes. "This weakening. Once it begins, does it go fast?"

"I can't tell you that. Every case varies. It could take one month or ten, but you may want to come out here to see her within the next few weeks."

Nina didn't have to look at her calendar to know that the next few weeks were fully booked. This was her busy season. A trip to Omaha would take precious time, not to mention a toll on her emotions. Seeing her mother was always painful. "Why don't I talk with you next week and see how she is then," she suggested. "If she stays stabilized, I'd rather wait a bit before coming out."

The doctor agreed to that, as Nina knew he would. Though the home was the finest Nina had been able to find, it wasn't unlike others in its overriding concern with money. Nina paid well for the service of having her mother cared for. As long as the checks kept coming, Anthony Kimball and his staff were content.

Hanging up the phone, Nina felt the same hollow ache she felt whenever she thought of her mother. Such potential gone to waste. A beautiful woman now a vegetable. She wished she could credit the damage to a disease like Alzheimer's, but her mother's mind hadn't fallen victim to anything as noble as that. She'd taken drugs. Bad drugs. Too many drugs. Rather than dying of an overdose, she had lived on, simply to languish in whatever position her attendants arranged her.

Nina was the one who felt the pain of it all. She was the one who felt the remorse. She couldn't say that she felt a loss, because her mother had never been hers to enjoy, but there were times, once in a very great while, when she thought of what might have been if things had been different way back at the start.

But they wouldn't be—couldn't be—and thinking about it only caused pain. One of Nina's earliest lessons in life had been that the only sure antidote to pain was activity. It was a lesson she still lived by.

4

SUNDAY WAS MOVING DAY. Nina completed all her weekend showings on Saturday and was up with the sun the next morning to pack the last of her things. Rather than pay a formal moving service, when she had so little of intrinsic value to move, she had hired two young men to help. Between their muscles, the small pickup truck one of them owned and the promise of a generous check for the job, they had successfully transferred her meager furnishings and not so meager personal belongings from the old apartment to the new one by noon.

Shortly after, Nina went to work, first pushing the furniture over or back until the positioning was perfect, then opening carton after carton in an attempt to see what was where. She was standing in the midst of chaos, feeling vaguely bewildered, when she heard a call from downstairs.

"Hello?"

She tried to place it, but she wasn't expecting any guests. "Yes?" she called back without moving.

"It's John Sawyer, Nina. Can I come up?"

"Uh—" she looked around, bewildered, "—sure." John Sawyer? Downstairs? She hadn't seen hide nor hair of him since the Tuesday before, and though she told herself to be grateful, more than once she had wondered where he was. The consortium wanted them to work together, but since she wasn't thrilled with the idea, she'd decided to leave the initiative up to him. She hadn't expected that he'd seek her out in person, much less at her home, much *less* at the home whose exact address he couldn't possibly have known.

Yet John Sawyer it was emerging from the stairwell wearing a T-shirt, jeans and sneakers. His hair was mussed, his nose and cheeks unexpectedly ruddy. He looked fresh and carefree, neither of which she was feeling at that moment, and as if that weren't bad enough, the first thing he did after he came to a halt was to give her an ear-to-ear grin.

John had never grinned at her before. She'd caught a twist of the corner of the mouth once or twice, but never a full-fledged grin. The surprise of it had her insides doing little flip-flops, to which she responded by frowning.

"How did you find me?"

"Your car. You said you were moving to Sycamore Street. There aren't many houses here with bright red BMWs in the driveway."

For reasons unknown to Nina just then, she felt suddenly defensive about the car. "It's not new. I bought it used and had it painted. Some people think it's pretentious to have a car like that when I live pretty modestly, but the fact is that it impresses clients. They like riding around in it."

John studied her, his grin softening into something curious. "Don't you?"

"Don't I what?"

"Like riding around in it."

"I suppose." She frowned again. "What are you doing here?"

"Helping." He stuck his hands into the back pockets of his jeans, a gesture that should have been totally innocent. Given the way his T-shirt tightened over his chest, though, it wasn't. Nina felt a corresponding tightening in the pit of her stomach.

"I told you I didn't need help," she snapped, scowling now.

"Everyone needs help." His eyes skimmed the sea of cartons on the floor. "This place will be a mess until everything's unpacked. Why be burdened doing it after work every day this week, when between the two of us, we can get it all done now?"

He had a point, though she wouldn't concede it. "I'm sure you have better things to do with your time."

"Actually, I don't. J.J. and I were at the beach this morning, but he's gone off for the afternoon with friends, and the store is closed, so I really do have time to waste. I'm in the mood for unpacking." Shifting his hands from his pockets to his hips, he looked around at the cartons. "Where should I begin?"

"Uh—" Nina tried to concentrate, but all she could think about was that she hadn't showered, that she hadn't put makeup on and that between her ultrashort hair and the loose shirt and jeans she wore, she looked more like a boy than a girl. She felt embarrassed. "Uh, really, John, there's no need—"

"Where?" he repeated. Stepping over one carton, he peered down to look at the writing on the side of another. The words *living room* had been crossed out and replaced by *dining room*, but that, too, had been crossed out. *Bedroom* was the word that seemed left, though even from where she was, Nina saw through the open flaps of the box that it contained pots and pans.

"I've used these cartons lots of different times," she explained, wringing one hand in the other. "I kind of gave up on marking things this time, which is why everything's mixed up out here."

"No sweat," John said, lifting the carton. "This looks like it goes in the kitchen." He hitched his chin toward the back of the house. "That way?"

"Uh-huh."

Carrying the carton, he passed her, went through the dining room and into the kitchen. Within minutes, she heard the clattering of pots and pans being stacked. Wondering where he was putting them, she followed the noise to find him on his haunches before one of the kitchen cabinets. "I don't know if this is right, but at least they'll be out of the way. If you find in a week or a month that you want them elsewhere, it'll be easy enough to move them."

"That's fine."

"Why don't you go back into the other room and sort through the rest of the cartons. If I carry stuff into the bedroom, you can organize things there, while I finish up here."

She tried again. "John, this really isn't necessary."

"Of course, it's not. But it helps, doesn't it?"

Given the direct question, she couldn't lie. "Yes, but—"

"Unless there's stuff here you don't want me to see."

"There isn't, but—"

"Or you're expecting someone else and my being here will embarrass you—"

"I'm not and it won't, but—"

"Then there's no problem."

"There *is* a problem," she cried, driven by exasperation to a semblance of her usual force. "I told you this last week. If I wanted help, I'd hire it."

He looked up at her. "And pay for it. With a check. Yes, I did hear that."

"Well, I meant it."

His eyes held hers for a time before he returned them to the task at hand. He had barely set another pot into the nest of them in the cabinet when he looked up again. "This is free, Nina. I'm not asking for payment of any kind, and if you offered, I'd give it back. I'm doing this as a friend. You won't owe me anything."

She felt color warm her cheeks. "I know that."

"I'm not sure you do," he said with a frown. "You've made it clear that you prefer to hire and pay people when you need things done. But when you get someone who's willing to help for free, the only reason I can think of why you'd turn him down is that either you can't stand his company or you're afraid there's a price." His words came slowly but steadily, one sentence flowing gently into the next. "Now, I know we haven't necessarily hit it off on a personal basis, so it may well be that you can't stand my company, and if that's the case, just tell me, and I'll leave. On the other hand, if you're afraid there's a price, I'm telling you there isn't. I'm offering my services free and clear of return obligations." He paused. "Do you believe me?"

After a minute, she said a quiet, "Yes."

"Then why don't you let me help." It was more statement than question. "Come on, Nina. Go with the flow. I'm here and I'm willing. Use me."

Use me. It was usually the other way around, where relationships between men and women were concerned. But he'd said the words himself. He'd offered them. Freely. Just as he was offering his help. "Are you sure you don't have anything else to do?"

"I'm sure."

As he sat there on his haunches looking up at her, it struck Nina that he wasn't bad looking. Not bad looking at all. Actually, rather good-looking, even with those glasses perched on his nose. With his longish hair, his light tan, and his T-shirt and jeans, the glasses made him look oddly in vogue.

Which was a surprising thought, indeed.

"Fine," she said, and headed for the front room before she had a chance to regret the decision. "I'll sort through the cartons. Come back in when you need another one."

With a certain amount of kicking and shoving, she had cartons separated into groups by the time John returned. As promised, he carried everything for the bedroom into the bedroom before continuing with the kitchen.

For one hour, then a second, they worked straight. Nina was back to being her usual efficient self, in part to keep her mind occupied and away from the fact of John's presence in the other room. Come the time when they were both unpacking cartons in the living room, that became more difficult. He was never out of sight. She was highly aware of him. Adding to the problem, most of the cartons contained books, so John's progress slowed. For every four that he placed on the shelf, there was one that he wanted to discuss.

She tried to keep moving. She tried, even when she was giving her opinion of one book or another, to keep unloading others and lining them up on the shelves. But the questions he asked were good ones, often ones that required thought, and she found her own progress slowing down right along with his. She found herself curious to know *his* opinions.

Nina had never thought of herself as an intellectual. She had a college degree more out of practical necessity than love of learning. John, on the other hand, was an intellectual. It was clear in the way he looked and acted, not to mention his occupation, and to some extent, she had assumed that given this difference between them, they would have trouble communicating. To her surprise, they didn't. He didn't make obscure references to classical writers or philosophers. He didn't pick apart books along the lines of arcane theories. He offered honest, straightforward thoughts in honest, straightforward English. Pleasantly surprised, she indulged herself the discussion, letting her defenses down, enjoying the talk for talk's sake.

Engrossed as she was in it, she was taken off guard when, in the midst of a discussion of James Joyce and his wife, Nora, John said, "Have you had lunch?"

Sitting cross-legged on the floor, she straightened, looked at him, swallowed. Dragging herself back from a pleasant interlude to the present, she glanced at her watch. "It's after three."

"I know. I'm starved. Did you have anything?"

Silently she shook her head.

"I'll go get something." Coming to his knees, he fished his keys from his pocket. With another smooth motion, he was on his feet. "You'll eat, won't you?"

"I don't need—"

"Are you hungry?"

"I wasn't planning to—"

"Lobster rolls?"

Her mouth watered. "Only if I pay."

He thought about that for a minute. She was prepared to dig in her heels and insist that that was the only way she'd eat anything he brought, when his mouth quirked. "Okay."

He was *quite* good-looking, she realized with a start. Dragging her eyes from his, she looked around for her purse. Unfortunately, it was directly behind him. The only footpath through the cartons took her by him with mere inches to spare. His flesh was warm from work. She felt that warmth, smelled its scent, and where she should have been repelled, she wasn't. John Sawyer smelled healthily male. Attractively male.

Convinced that the tension of the move was jumbling her mind, she quickly found her purse and fumbled inside her enough money to cover sandwiches and drinks. John took the money.

"You do know," he said, and eyed her straight on, "that I'd never allow this if it weren't for the big deal you made about not wanting my help to unpack. The way I see it, your treating me now is payment for my work, so we're even. Got that?"

His gaze was so strong and his voice so firm that all she could do was manage a quiet, "Uh-huh." If he had asked her to say anything else, she'd have been at a loss. Fortunately, he didn't. Tucking the money into his pocket, he went off down the stairs.

During the time he was gone, Nina was a whirling dervish of activity. Bending over and around repeatedly, she emptied two full cartons of books, then moved on to her stereo equipment. She tried not to think about anything but the work she was doing, and to some extent she succeeded. Only intermittently did images flash through her mind—John's long arms flexing under the weight of cartons, John's shaggy hair spiking along his neck, John's very male, very alluring scent—but she pushed them away as quickly as they came.

She had a rack of CDs filled and was halfway through a second when he returned.

"This is a treat, let me tell you," he said with a smile as he began to unload the bag he carried. Shifting a carton from the low coffee table onto the floor, he spread out not only lobster rolls, but cups of potato salad, ears of corn and soda. "Take-out for me is usually McDonald's."

Instinctively Nina knew that the choice had nothing to do with money. "That's what your son likes?"

"He *loves* it. He'd be happy to go there every day of the week if I let him."

"What does he eat?"

"A hamburger, a small bag of fries and a milk shake. He doesn't always make it through the shake, but he devours the rest. For a little guy, he always amazes me."

"He's four?"

John nodded. Sitting down on a nearby carton, stretching his legs comfortably before him, he took a bite of a lobster roll, closed his eyes, chewed softly and neatly. "Mmm," he said with feeling, "is this good."

Nina, too, took a carton as a seat. Using one of the plastic forks that had tumbled from the bag, she sampled the potato salad. "So's this." She took another bite, all the while thinking about her curiosity and the fact that maybe, now that she and John were friends, she could ease it. It seemed she'd been wondering about certain things for a long time.

Shooting for nonchalance, she took a sip of soda, then said, "Tell me about your son."

John's glasses might have hidden the flash of wariness in his eyes had she not been watching him closely. Clearly he guarded his son. She wondered if he'd tell her to mind her own business—one part of her was telling herself that very same thing—and felt deeply warmed when, instead, he said in a low, slow voice, "J.J.'s a sweet little boy who's had a rough go of it in life."

"When did his mom die?"

"When he was one. He doesn't remember her."

"Is that good or bad?"

"Good, I guess. He doesn't know what he's missing."

Nina wanted to ask how the woman had died, but didn't. It was enough that John had agreed to talk about his son. "I'm sure you give him twice the love."

"I try," he said thoughtfully, and took another mouthful of lobster roll. After he'd swallowed, he said, "It's hard sometimes knowing if what I'm doing is right. Normal guidelines don't fit when it comes to J.J. He's a special child."

Eating her own lobster roll, she waited for him to go on. As curious as she was, she didn't want to sound nosy. Surprisingly the silence wasn't awkward. She ate patiently, wondering about all those ways in which J.J. might be special.

Finally John raised his eyes to hers. "What have you heard about him?"

"Just that he has vision and hearing deficiencies."

"That's pretty much it. He wears glasses and hearing aids." With the words, John looked momentarily in pain. "God, it hurts to see him sometimes. My heart aches for the poor little kid. He didn't ask for any of this."

"What caused it?"

He thought about that for a minute, then shrugged. "No one knows. He was born that way."

"Did you know right then?"

He shook his head. "Things seemed fine at the beginning. By the time he was six months old, I could tell that he wasn't responding to sound. It was when I brought him in to be tested that they detected the problem with his eyes. Unfortunately, there wasn't much of a medical nature that they could do about either. They wouldn't even fit him for glasses until he was close to a year. He'd have just dragged them off."

"They must help."

He nodded. "A lot. He reads."

"At four?"

John shot her a quintessentially parent-proud grin. "Nothing's wrong with his mind. He's a bright little kid."

"I'm sure," Nina said.

"I wasn't. Given all the other problems, I'd been told there was a possibility that he'd be retarded. Thank goodness that isn't so. I mean, how much should the child have to take?"

"But you'll be putting him in a special school." That was what she'd been told, the major reason John had invested in Crosslyn Rise. Handled wisely over the years, the profit he stood to make would cover the high cost of that special school.

"I have to. What hearing he has is negligible. He has to learn how to sign, how to read lips and how to talk."

"That'll all start next year?"

"It all started as soon as we diagnosed the problem. He and I work with a therapist every morning, and in the afternoon he's in a play group with children like him. Their parents are trained like I am. The learning for these kids has to be continuous." His eyes widened and he shot a hurried glance at his watch. The abrupt movement, coming from him, took Nina by surprise. Seeing the time, he let out a breath. "I'm okay. He's with one of those other families today, but I still have a few minutes."

"Oh, John, I feel guilty. It can't be often that you get a free afternoon like this, and to blow it away unpacking my things. I'm really sorry."

He regarded her strangely. "Don't be. If I hadn't wanted to do this, I wouldn't have. You didn't exactly invite me." He paused. "You didn't exactly *want* me. I inflicted myself on you, so you don't have anything to feel guilty about." He paused again. "Besides, I got a lobster roll out of it. And some interesting conversation." His voice lowered. "I like you better when you're talking books than when you're talking real estate."

"The feeling's mutual," Nina said, then regretted it the moment the words were out because, behind his glasses, John's eyes darkened. "You're not as bad as I thought you'd be," she added quickly, lest he think she was being suggestive in any way, shape or form.

His eyes remained dark. They dropped to her mouth.

"I think," she babbled on, "that when you only see a person in one context, say for matters involving a business deal like Crosslyn Rise, you get a very narrow view." Her voice seemed to be fading, like the rest of her was doing. Fading, weakening, feeling all warm and trembly inside. "It's nice to know you like lobster rolls."

John's brows drew together in a brief frown before he managed to drag his eyes back to hers. "I do," he said quietly. "But I'd better go, I think." He stood.

Simply so that she wouldn't feel so overwhelmed, Nina stood, too. "Thanks." She waved a hand in the vague direction of the food, then broadened the gesture. "For everything."

He walked slowly to the door, one hand deep in his pocket reaching for his keys, his head slightly bent.

Nina was suddenly nervous. "John? I didn't upset you, asking about your son, did I?"

"No, no." He pulled the keys from his pocket, but he didn't turn.

She moved closer. "I was curious. That's all."

They keys jangled in his hands. "People are."

She moved closer still. "You must be a very good parent. I'm beginning to feel a little humbled."

"That makes two of us."

She frowned. "Two?"

Slowly he turned, and what she saw in his eyes took her breath away. His voice was low, still slow but nowhere near as smooth as it usually was. "I thought I was immune to women like you. I thought that there was no way a woman with a fast-driving career could turn me on, but I was wrong."

A tiny voice inside Nina told her she ought to be angry, to either lash back or turn in the opposite direction and run, but that voice was drowned out by the sound of her pulse beating rapidly, hammering her feet in place on the floor.

His hand shaped her cheek, then slid along her jaw until his fingers were feathered by her hair. "Tell me not to want to kiss you," he said.

But she couldn't. As outlandish as it seemed, given that John Sawyer was the antithesis of the kind of man she usually liked, she wanted his kiss. Maybe, deep down inside, she'd been wanting it since he'd shown up at her door that afternoon wearing a T-shirt that made his chest look heart-stoppingly hard and broad. Maybe she'd been wanting it even longer, since the night she'd shown up at his store and seen him sweating. There was something about sweat that blew the intellectual image. Sweat was earthy and honest. Sweat was intimate. Given the right chemistry between a man and a woman, it was a powerful aphrodisiac.

Whether she wanted it to be so or not, Nina had to accept that the chemistry between John and her was right. There was no way her body was letting her move away from his touch, no way it was letting her evade him when his head slowly lowered and his mouth touched hers.

He gave her one kiss, then a second, then a third. Each one lasted a little longer than the one before, each one touched her a little more deeply. He seemed to be savoring her, reluctantly, if his words were to be considered, but savoring her nonetheless. His lips were firm, knowing, increasingly open and wet. His kisses were smooth as warm butter and ten times more hot.

By the time the last one ended and he raised his head, Nina's breath was coming in short, shallow wisps. Her eyes were closed. She felt miles and miles away from everything she'd always known, transported to a place where kisses touched the heart. She'd never been there before.

"I shouldn't have done that," he said quietly.

She opened her eyes to find his face flushed, his eyes serious. "Probably not," she said softly.

"You're not my type."

"Nor you mine."

"So why did it happen?"

She tried to think up an eloquent answer, but for all the hard selling she'd done in her day, she was without one. The best she could do was to murmur, "Chemistry?"

After a minute's thought, he said, "I guess." As though the admission were a warning, he passed his thumb over her lips—moist now, warm and naturally rouged—before letting his hand fall to his side.

"I didn't come here for this," he said gruffly. "I hope you know that."

She did. Somehow, with John, it wouldn't have occurred to her otherwise. He wasn't a wily sort of man.

"I'm not looking for anything," he went on, still in that same gruff voice. "I don't have time for this kind of thing. Between the store and my son, I have all I can handle."

"Hey," she said, taking a step back, "I'm not asking for anything." It sounded to her as though he thought she was, or would. "It wasn't *me* who started that kiss."

"You didn't tell me to stop."

"Because I was curious about it. But it's no big thing. It's over and done. Curiosity satisfied. Period."

He thought about that, then nodded. But he didn't turn to leave. Instead, he looked thoughtful again. Then, in a low voice, he said, "Was it good?"

She took a deep breath. "You don't really want to know."

"I want to know."

"It won't help the situation."

"I want to know."

"It'll only make you angry, because the last thing you want is for someone like me to say it was good."

"Was it?"

"John," she pleaded, "why don't you just leave it be?"

"Because I want to know," he said with the stubbornness of a child. Nina had the sudden fear that he would stand there asking until she told him the truth.

Staring him in the eye, she said, "Yes, it was good. It was very good, and I'm sorry it ended. But it had to, because it wasn't right. We're totally different people with totally different wants and needs. You can't understand why I talk so fast, and I can't understand why you talk so slow. I want to make money, you want to meditate on the beach." Her hands went in opposite directions. "Worlds apart, John, we're worlds apart."

"Yeah." His amber eyes moved over her features. "It's too bad. You're awful cute."

She snorted. "Cute is what every woman over thirty wants to be."

"Over thirty?"

"Thirty-one, to be exact."

His mouth quirked at the corner. "I wouldn't have guessed it."

That quirking annoyed her. She didn't like being laughed at. "Well, now you know, and since you do, you can understand that I mean all I say about what I'm doing and where I'm going. I'm not some cute little pixie fresh out of college trying to make it big. I've had years of training in my field, and now that I'm on the verge of getting where I want to be, I'm not letting anyone stand in my way." She stole in a breath and raced on. "So if you think that I'm going to think twice about that kiss, that I'm going to look for a replay or want something *more*, you're mistaken. I'm off and running, and you'll only slow me down. I won't let that happen."

Having said her piece in a way that she felt was forceful and clear, she stood her ground with her jaw set, waiting for John to do his thinking thing then come up with a rejoinder. Not more than thirty seconds had passed, though, when, with a start, he glanced at his watch.

"Damn," he muttered, "I'm late." Raising his arm in a wave, he was fast out the door, taking the stairs at a speedy trot. Nina had never seen him move so fast, but it made sense that if he did it for anyone, he would do it for his son, and she was glad. From what he said, the boy had precious little going for him but a good brain and a loving dad.

Standing there amid the cartons in the living room that didn't feel quite hers yet, Nina's mind traveled back in time to when she'd been four herself. She hadn't had any obvious handicap. Her vision had been fine, along with her hearing, and her mind had been sharp—too sharp, in some respects. Even at that age she had wondered why she didn't have a father. Even then she had known something was wrong when she'd heard gruff voices coming from her mother's room late at night. Even then she had known that the bruises on her mother's face and arms and legs weren't normal.

She sighed. Ignorance would have been bliss back then, but what was done was done. She'd overcome those things that had darkened her early years and was now well on her way to having the security she wanted. Okay, so once in a while she wished things were different. Once in a while she wished *she* had someone rush home to her the way John Sawyer had to his son. But life wasn't perfect, she knew. No one had everything. So if she didn't have that special someone who cared, she had a growing career and a growing name and lots of respect along the way. She could live with that. She had no other choice.

COME EIGHT O'CLOCK that night, she wasn't thinking of choices. Having unpacked the very last carton, the only thing on her mind was soaking in a hot, hot bath. Stripping out of her shirt and jeans, she started the water and returned to the bedroom for a robe, when the phone rang.

Absurdly, her first thought was that the phone would also be ringing at her old apartment, jangling through rooms now empty and forlorn. Remembering the good two years she'd had there, she felt a twinge of sadness.

Her second thought was that Lee was calling in to report on any activity that had taken place at the office that day. Shrugging into the robe, she reached for the phone.

"Hello?"

"Nina?"

It was a man's voice. Though she hadn't ever heard it before on the phone, she knew instantly whose it was. Thoughts of him had been hovering at the back of her mind since he'd left her house in such a rush.

"Hi," she said cautiously.

"It's John."

"I know."

The line was silent for a time before he said, "I, uh, just wanted to apologize for leaving so abruptly. Time had gotten away from me and J.J. was due home."

"Did you get back in time?"

"Almost."

"No?"

"They were waiting out front in the car."

"For long?"

"Three or four minutes. I'm usually on time. They were starting to worry."

"How about J.J.?"

"He was okay."

"Did he have fun?"

"I think so. Sometimes it's hard to tell whether he had a good time or he's just real happy to be home. One thing's for sure. He ate enough. He was wearing mustard, fruit punch and chocolate all over his shirt."

"Oh, yuck." She thought about single parenthood, and a sudden fear struck. "Are you the one who has to do the wash?"

"You got it."

"Oh, *yuck*."

"Actually, given all I've had to clean up in the last four years, the dribbles from a picnic lunch are a snap."

Nina found herself picturing those other things. "You changed diapers?"

"All the time."

"What a good father. And husband. Your wife must have appreciated that." Once the words were out, she held her breath.

"Actually," he said after a brief pause, "she took it pretty much for granted. It was part of the bargain we made. I wanted the baby. She agreed to carry it if I was willing to take the responsibility for its care once it was born."

"That's awful," Nina exclaimed without thinking, then she did think and regretted the outburst. If John had adored his now-dead wife, the last thing Nina wanted to do was criticize her. "I mean, I suppose people do what's right for them. Did it work for her?"

"Not particularly. She went right back to work the way she planned, but she felt guilty, and she resented that."

"Oh, dear."

"Yeah." He paused. "Well." Another pause, then a new breath. "Anyway, I'm used to doing everything for J.J. It's kind of fun. Gives me a real sense of self-sufficiency."

Nina thought about that. "Do you cook?"

"Nothing gourmet, but he doesn't mind that. He's big on things like BLTs, and PB and Fs."

"PB and Fs?"

"Peanut butter and fluff sandwiches. Not quite the kind of meal you make, I'm sure."

Remembering the exchange they'd had over cookbooks in his store, Nina felt sheepish. "I don't really do that much."

"Ha," he scoffed. "I'm the one who unpacked your kitchen today. I saw that wok and that clay pot and that fondue dish."

"Those are all for fun. I don't use them often, except maybe for the wok. When I want a quick meal and don't feel like a frozen dinner, I stir-fry something up. I'm pretty good at it, actually. I've found some good recipes. I'll make you something sometime, if you'd like."

For the third time in the conversation, words had slipped from her mouth that she hadn't consciously put there. The idea that John Sawyer, whom she worked with but with whom she didn't have another thing in common except a love for reading, should want to come back to her house—for dinner, no less—was ridiculous. Surely he'd see that.

"Yeah," he said, "well, maybe." He paused. "So. Did you finish with the rest of your things?"

Feeling as though she'd been eased from a precarious place, she said, "Sure did. I'm feeling it now."

"Sore?"

"Mmm. I was just about to get in the—oh, hell! Hold on! I forgot about the water!" All but dropping the phone on the floor, she raced into the bathroom in time to watch the first of a steaming waterfall cascade over the edge of the tub. Frantically twisting the taps, she turned off the water, pulled out the plug, then reached for the towels she'd so recently hung on the nearby bar. "Good show, Nina," she muttered to herself as she mopped up the spillage. When she had the worst of it absorbed, she dropped the sodden towels into the sink, replaced the plug with just enough water left for her bath and returned to the phone.

"I can't believe I did that," she said without prelude. "A fine thing it'd be if the first night I'm here, I send water dripping onto my landlord's head."

"All cleaned up?"

"Enough." Thinking of the still-damp floor, she sighed. "I'd better go finish. Thanks for calling, John. And thanks again for your help. It was nice."

Some time later, lying in the tub with the heat of the water seeping into her tired limbs, Nina realized that it had been nice, both his help and his call. He was a nice man. A *sexy* man. All wrong for her, of course, and there was no point in even *thinking* of a repeat of that kiss. Still, he was nice to be with—which was what she told Lee the next morning when she was asked about the car that had been parked behind her car that Sunday afternoon.

"I was going to stop in and see how you were doing," Lee explained, "but when I saw that, I figured you already had a guest. I never thought it'd be John Sawyer." Her eyes narrowed in play. "Is there something you haven't told me?"

"Nothing at all," Nina said, cool and composed from the top of her shiny black hair to the toes of her shiny purple shoes. "John Sawyer is someone I work with. He knew I was moving, so he stopped by to help."

"I thought he drove you nuts."

"He does when it comes to work. But he's good for lifting cartons. So I used him." More pointedly she said, "That's what you have to learn to do. Turn the tables on Tom. Use him for a change, rather than the other way around."

"I'm not moving."

"Then use him for something else. Ask him to bring the wine and dessert if you're the one who's cooking dinner. Ask him to give you a lift to the service station when you have to pick up your car."

Lee wrinkled her nose. "I don't think he'd appreciate that."

"Probably not." Her voice gentled. "He does things on his terms, and his terms alone. That's not good. It's not fair."

Lee shrugged. "Maybe not, but that's the way it is."

Not for me, Nina thought. *Never for me.* She had her work. It, and the reward it brought, were all she needed.

With that reminder, she swiveled around to face her computer, punched up the current listings and got busy.

5

Out of sight was not out of mind. Nina tried not to think about John. She tried not to think about the way he looked or the way he acted. Mostly she tried not to think about the way he kissed, but it didn't work. Memory was insidious, wending through her mind in brief but potent flashes.

She hadn't had a kiss like that since...she'd *never* had a kiss like that. In her experience, men kissed women either rapaciously, showing their hunger and proud of it, or timidly, showing their fear, hoping to pass it off as sensitivity. John hadn't kissed her either of those ways. His kiss had been forceful in a quiet, thoughtful way, which was pretty much how he was himself. He'd known what he was doing. His mouth had conveyed the attraction he felt. The fact that the attraction was unbidden made it all the more special.

But it was over, and she had put it from her mind, so she immersed herself in her work for all she was worth. It wasn't hard, since she loved what she did. And there was plenty to keep her busy. If she wasn't out showing a piece of property, she was working with the newspaper on fresh copy or doing paperwork for an impending sale or tracking down a competitor with a co-broke offer. When she was in the office, her phone was forever ringing.

None of those calls were from John. As the week wore on, during those brief in-between times when she thought of him, she began to wonder why he hadn't called. He had been so persistent at first that they discuss Crosslyn Rise, and though the decision on pricing had been made, the consortium had very clearly asked them to continue to work together.

She wondered whether he was as bothered, after the fact, by that kiss as she was.

She wondered whether he was embarrassed. Or disappointed. Or disgusted.

She wondered whether he hated her.

By Friday afternoon, she'd just about had it with the wondering. Picking up the phone, she punched out his number.

He answered, his voice deep and pleasantly resonant. "The Leaf Turner."

"John? It's Nina. Am I getting you at a bad time?" Heart pounding, she waited.

His voice came back a little less deep than it had been. "No, not at all. There's actually a comfortable lull here right now. How are you?"

She chose to believe he was pleased that she'd called. "Fine," she answered lightheartedly. "And you?"

"Can't complain."

"How's J.J.?" she asked, knowing it was the one thing that would guarantee a positive response.

"Great. The girls took him out for ice cream. He loves that."

"Girls, plural?"

"Two. Twins. What with J.J.'s problems, I like knowing there are two of them, so that one can keep an eye on him at any given time. You know how baby-sitters can be."

Actually she didn't. An only child herself, she'd never had a baby-sitter, but had been left with a neighbor or, at a frighteningly tender age, alone. Her mother hadn't had the money to pay a sitter. By virtue of that same fact, when Nina had been old enough to work, she had bypassed baby-sitting in favor of a supermarket job with more regular hours and higher pay. It hadn't mattered that the supermarket didn't hire kids under fifteen. She had talked them into hiring her. Even back then, she'd had a persuasive mouth.

"Do they talk on the phone a lot?" she asked.

"It's not as much that, as getting distracted cooking pizza or watching television. Actually, these two are pretty responsible. And they think J.J. is adorable."

"I'll bet he is," Nina said, because if he looked anything like John, she was sure he was. "Did you get all the mustard and stuff out?"

"The what? Oh, that. Pretty much."

Again she pictured him doing the wash and felt admiration. He was a good father. A good man.

Aware of the silence, she cleared her throat and said, "Uh, I'm actually calling about work, John. I picked up the finished brochures from the printer today. They're the ones we'll be handing out at the open house, and then, after that, in the office to anyone interested in Crosslyn Rise. I thought you might like to see them."

"That would be nice," he said with what she could have sworn was a touch of caution.

"I'll be working most of the weekend, so I'll be in and out, but I have to man the front desk at the office Sunday morning from ten to twelve." She had thought it all out. Her calling him was a business move. She didn't want him thinking it was anything else. Hence, the office. "Do you want to stop by then?"

After a pause, he said, "I could do that."

"You could bring J.J. if you want." He certainly didn't have to hire a sitter for something as innocent as a brief office meeting. "We won't be long. You'll probably want to take the brochure home to study. I'll be passing out copies to all of the members of the consortium at our next meeting, but I thought you might want to see it before then. There may be some things that you think are stronger or weaker, that we can compensate for in person at the open house."

"Okay. I'll drop by."

"Sometime between ten and twelve?"

"Uh-huh."

She shrugged. That was that. "See you then."

SHE TOLD HERSELF that it was nothing more than another business meeting and probably wouldn't last longer than two minutes, still she took care in dressing, again passing over some of the more outlandish of her outfits in favor of a relatively sedate slacks set. Granted, the pants were harem-style and the top short and loose, but the color was moss green, the neck barely scooped and the sleeves as voluminous as the legs.

Well, hell, he didn't expect that she'd dress like a schoolmarm, did he? At least, the outfit wasn't neon pink, like some of hers were, and her nails weren't red now, but beige.

Ten o'clock came and went. She talked with a couple who walked in off the street, people who thought *maybe* they'd look for something new but *only* if they could sell their old place and what were their chances of that. Ten-fifteen became ten-thirty. One of Martin's clients came by to drop some papers he'd signed. A potential buyer called to check on the time of another open house. Ten forty-five passed and eleven arrived.

She was beginning to wonder whether he'd forgotten, when, shortly before eleven-thirty, he came leisurely through the door. He was alone; she felt an unexpected stab of disappointment at that. But the disappointment was brief, because he looked so good. His hair was damp, freshly combed back over his ears and down over his nape. He was wearing a white shirt—open at the neck, with the sleeves rolled—and a pair of jeans that looked relatively new. She wondered if it was his Sunday best.

When he planted himself directly before her desk, she smiled. "You've been at the beach again." His skin had a golden glow, a bit of new color over what she'd seen the week before.

He nodded. "This morning. J.J. is still there."

Her face dropped. "Oh, I'm sorry, John. I didn't mean to drag you away from him. This wasn't so important. We could have done it another time."

"You didn't drag me away. He's with friends. He's happy."

"The same friends who took him out last week?"

He shook his head. "Different ones. They have a daughter with special needs. She's just about J.J.'s age. They're in the same play group."

"Do all the children in the play group have similar handicaps?"

"Roughly."

"How many children?"

"Twelve."

She was stunned. "And they all live around here?" She couldn't imagine so many four-year-olds with similar problems in the immediate area. As populations went, the local tally was low.

"No. Some of them come from pretty far, which means that we go pretty far to see them in return. But it's worth it. Socialization is critical, but it's hard for kids like these to get it through regular channels. I tried J.J. in a local play group when he was two. I figured that he was doing all the same things the other kids were, playing with blocks and all. But he wasn't talking. Since he couldn't hear, he couldn't react to the other kids the way they expected. And he made the mothers nervous."

Nina thought that was awful. "Screw *them*."

He gave a lopsided grin that created a dimple in his cheek—and sent a ripple of awareness through Nina. "I felt the same way. Actually, I felt worse. I was furious. Then I thought about it, and I talked it over with J.J.'s therapists, and the way we reasoned it out, it wasn't so awful. Those women were nervous because they didn't know how to communicate with J.J. They kept expecting him to be just like their own kids, only he wasn't. Isn't. And it didn't matter how angry I got, no way was that experience going to be positive, and that's the name of the game. So now he's with people who understand him. They understand me. We've all been through the same things. We help each other."

"Like watching kids at the beach?"

"Like that."

Nina reached for the brochure that she'd tucked safely to the side. "You'll probably want to take this and leave, then." She held it out, trying to be a good sport. "It's a beautiful day for the beach. You'll be anxious to get back."

He closed his hand around it, but rather than turning away, he arched a questioning brow toward the chair by the desk. She was surprised, and delighted. With an enthusiastic, "Please," she watched him lower himself into the chair, stretch out his legs and open the brochure.

He really *was* handsome, she decided again. He wasn't urbane or sophisticated looking, certainly not slick, still he was handsome. Today there was something western about him. With his fresh jeans and his damp hair and the color the sun had painted on his skin, he looked like a cowboy newly off the range and showered. With high-heeled boots, the picture would have been complete. Then again, she preferred his deck shoes, particularly the way he wore them without socks. She wondered what his ankles were like, whether they were as well formed as his hands and wrists, and half wished he'd cross one of his legs so she could see.

But he didn't. Looking perfectly comfortable as he was, he took his time reading the copy, studying the drawings, closing the brochure to look at the piece as a whole. "This is very professional," he said at last.

She felt inordinately pleased. "Thank you. Do you think it'll impress the people we want to impress?"

"It should." He turned to the last page, where the price guides were listed. "I was wondering whether they'd get these right."

"You mean, you were wondering whether I'd hike those prices back up between the time the consortium voted and the printer printed?" She couldn't quite tell if he was kidding. Rather than overreact if he was, she kept her voice light. "I wouldn't do that, John."

He shrugged. "You never can tell with typos."

"There aren't any typos in that brochure. Not a single one. I've been over it with a fine-tooth comb dozens of times. It's perfect."

Taking several more minutes, he looked through it again. Then, unfolding himself from the chair, he stood. "I like it, Nina."

She hated to see him leave so soon. "I thought maybe you'd have some suggestions."

"This is pretty much a *fait accompli*, isn't it?"

"Yes, it's all printed, but that doesn't mean we can't approach things differently when we're talking with clients, if you think a different approach is called for." She was feeling a little foolish, because he was right. The brochure was done and printed. Everything major was correct. To change something small and reprint hundreds of copies would be an absurd expense.

Still, the consortium wanted them to work together.

Eyes on the brochure, he said, "Why don't I take this home and read it again—" his voice dropped and slowed "—when I'm not so distracted by the piles of soft stuff you're wearing." With each of the last words, his eyes rose a notch until finally they met hers. "I'll call you if anything comes to mind."

She swallowed. "That sounds okay."

He nodded. Raising two fingers in a wave that could have been negligent, bashful or reluctant, he left.

NINA MADE A POINT not to wait for his call. She figured that after the way she'd invited him over when she could as well have put the brochure in the mail, a little aloofness was called for. So she ran around as usual, confident that if he called the office, she'd get his message, and that if he called her at home, he'd keep calling until she was there.

It wasn't until Thursday night that she picked up her phone in response to its ring and heard his voice. "I still think the brochure is fine," he said after the briefest of exchanged hellos. "But I thought maybe we could go up to the Rise and take a look around. I haven't been there in a while. If you're looking for the reaction of an everyday Joe, I'm your man."

Not even at the beginning, when Nina had broken into cold sweats over John's pokey ways, had she thought of him as an everyday Joe, and she certainly didn't now. He was different. He marched to his own drummer. She did concede, though, that of all the consortium members, he was probably the one to give the most off-the-cuff response, so she supposed in a way he was right.

"Okay. When can you go?"

"Tomorrow morning, actually, but I know this is pretty last-minute for you. You probably have appointments all over the place."

She did. She didn't have to dig out her appointment book to know that, and when she did open it, she saw that her schedule was even worse than she'd thought. But John was free, and he was right. They really should get up to see Crosslyn Rise.

"I may be able to shift things around," she said, her mind already at work. "Can you give me half an hour to find out?"

"Sure. I'll call back."

During the next thirty minutes, Nina phoned four clients, one other broker and Lee. By the time John called back, she had cleared a two-hour stretch starting at ten. They agreed to meet then.

NO MATTER HOW FREQUENT a visitor Nina was to the Rise, she was always amazed at the progress she found with each return. Most impressive this time was the mansion. It had long since been scooped clean of its innards, with little left but structural elements such as the grand staircase and period details like ceiling moldings and chair rails. Renovation was well under way. Woodwork that had been stripped and sanded was now being stained. Walls were being modified, doorways shifted from one spot to another. From the large first-floor room that would serve as an elegant paneled meeting-room-lounge-library, to the large back room that would be a health club, to the totally modernized kitchen, the two private dining rooms, and the charming suites on the second floor that could be rented out to guests, the place was suddenly taking on the feel of something on the verge of being real.

"Does this ever look different," John said as he stood with his head tipped back to take in the height of the huge front hall. "Very nice."

He wasn't bubbly. His voice was as quiet as ever. But Nina, who had studied his face closely in the recent past, could read the subdued excitement there. Taking excitement from that, she waved him on. "Come." She led him from one room to the next, pausing in the middle of each, letting the feel of the place seep in. At spots where there was active construction going on, they had to watch where they stepped and moved, and at those times, John either went first and took her arm to guide her by or cautioned her to take care.

Nina had never been one to cling to a man, but John's touch felt good. Particularly on bare skin. In deference to the June warmth, she had worn a sundress. It was bright yellow, actually little more than a long tank top that, once hiked up at the waist by a wide leather belt, grazed the top of her knees. She had also worn flats for the sake of walking, and the overall effect was to make her feel that much more delicate next to John, who, wearing jeans and an open-necked shirt—a horizontally striped one this time—looked surprisingly rugged.

She stayed close, under the guise of safety, until they reached the outdoors and the danger of flying wood chips was gone. She would have given him more room then, but he didn't move away. He stayed close by her side during the walk down the path toward the duck pond, where the first of the near-completed condos were.

"Such a gorgeous place," he said. "I don't know how Jessica was ever able to give it up."

"She had to. She couldn't keep it as it was, and we couldn't find a single seller who could afford the whole thing. So rather than seeing it broken down by a developer who didn't care a whit about the glory of the Rise, she decided to form the consortium and be the one to call the shots."

"Does she call them, or does Carter?"

Nina looked up to find a mischievous smile touching his mouth. Her gaze lingered on his mouth for a minute before she said, "Jessica does. Carter gives her input, and he runs the meetings, but in the end the decision is hers." She returned her eyes to the path.

"They seem happy."

"They are."

"I think she's pregnant."

Nina's eyes flew back to his. This time John seemed totally serious. "How do you know?"

"She has that look."

"You mean, radiance? For heaven's sake, John, that's a crock."

"It is not."

"When a woman is pregnant, she feels sick. Then fat and clunky. There's nothing radiant about being that way."

"Fine for you to say," John said, kicking aside a fallen twig. "You've never been pregnant. You don't know what the feeling's like."

She laughed. "And you do? I hate to tell you this, John—"

"I remember when my wife was pregnant," he said quietly. Coming to a stop, he looked off in the distance, seeing not the duck pond but another time years before. "She wasn't real happy about it, but I was. I thought it was a miracle, the idea of this little life growing inside her. Long before the baby moved, I could see the changes in her body. First her breasts, then her waist, nature doing its thing in a totally generic way. Maybe she was too close to be able to appreciate it. I was just that little bit removed, so I could see things in a broader scheme. Then, when I felt the baby move in her stomach, everything that had been so broad seemed to focus in on the fact that it was my child growing there." His breath caught on the intake. Seeming surprised by his own words, he looked quickly at Nina. "Sorry. I get carried away. It was an incredible experience."

Standing still beside him, she felt goose bumps running up and down her arms. "You make it sound incredible." And she could almost believe in radiance, because she could have sworn that was the look she had seen on John's face for the few seconds before he'd caught himself.

The look she saw now was more earthy, and there was no way his glasses could mask it. His eyes were on her goose bumps. "Cold?"

"No."

Lightly, starting at her wrists, he ran his hands up her arms. They stopped just shy of her shoulders to gently knead her skin. He watched their progress, first one, then the next. "It's too bad you don't want to have kids. You'd make a pretty mother."

Her skin felt hot where he touched it, and the heat was stealing inside. "People would have trouble telling me from the kids," she managed to say, though her voice was meager.

"Pregnant, I mean. You'd be pretty pregnant."

Her heart was racing. "Maybe more substantial."

"No." His eyes touched her breasts, which rose with each shallow breath she took. "You're substantial now. But it's different when you're pregnant. Not just added weight. Something else." His eyes slipped to her stomach, caressing it through the thin jersey material, causing the same kneading sensation that was so seductive on her arms. She could barely move, barely breathe. Slowly, searing a path along the way, his gaze rose and locked with hers. "I keep thinking about you, Nina. I don't want to, but I do."

At the reluctant admission, she started to shake her head, but he made a shushing motion with his mouth and that stopped her. His voice was low, slow and sandy. "I keep remembering that kiss. It was so good. The only problem was that nothing touched but our mouths."

"I know," she whispered.

While his hands kept up their gentle motion, his thumbs slid sensuously up and down under the thin straps at her shoulders. "I keep wondering what it would be like to touch other places. I lie in bed at night imagining. It's not fun."

She swallowed. "Because you don't want to like me?"

"Because I get hard."

Her breath caught in her throat and stayed there despite the wild skittering of her pulse. She gave a short, sharp shake of her head.

"What?"

"Don't say things like that," she begged.

"Because it embarrasses you?"

"Because it excites me."

The flare in John's eyes told her what her words had done. His thumbs began moving more widely, stroking her skin in small patches that inched downward, under the edge of her dress, over the starting swell of her breast.

"I want to touch you more," he said. With the lightest pressure, he brought her arms just that tiny bit forward to angle her body better for his seeking thumbs. They stroked deeper, even deeper, under her bra now, moving toward the center of her breasts.

Her nipples tightened. "John," she whispered weakly. Heat seemed to be gathering and pooling not only in her breasts, but down low. She clutched his hips for support.

"Let me," he whispered back, as his thumbs reached their twin goals. He circled them once, touched their tips, then moved back and forth in a gentle rubbing.

Catching in a small cry, Nina bit her lip. But the feeling in her breasts was still too intense, so she closed her eyes and dropped her head back.

With a low groan, John caught her to him. His hands left her breasts and circled her, drawing her fully into his body at the same time that his mouth came down on hers. He kissed her long and deep, first with his lips, then his tongue. Wrapping her arms around his neck, she sought his firmness. Opening her mouth wide to his, she tasted his hunger. There was nothing in him that was either rapacious or arrogant. He kissed her like a man who simply needed to be closer.

And closer he brought her. His arms swept over her back, one lower, one higher, pressing her into him at every point. His strength came at her through his thighs, his chest, his arms, made all the more enticing to her by the faint tremor that spoke of his restraint.

When he finally tore his mouth away, his breathing was ragged. Dragging his arms from around her, he took her face in his hands. "What the hell am I going to do with you?"

She didn't know what to say.

"Can you feel how much I want you?"

She hadn't been that long without a man that she didn't know the meaning of the hard presence against her stomach. Unable to take her eyes from his, she nodded.

"So?" he asked in frustration.

"So I don't sleep around."

"Me, neither."

"I don't take making love lightly."

"Me, neither.

"So we can't do it. We're all wrong for each other. We don't even like each other. And we have to work together."

He looked at her for a long time, his amber eyes dark and hungry still. "You're right." His thumbs skimmed her cheeks. "But all that doesn't take the wanting away. I haven't wanted a woman—"

He was cut off by the intrusion of a loud voice on the approach. "Okay, you guys, I think you'd better break it up."

Nina's head shot around as quickly as John's, and she found herself staring into the amused eyes of Carter Malloy, who was coming from the direction of the duck pond. Stopping not far from them, he said, "I think there's something about the air out here. It makes you forget that just anyone could be walking through. Fortunately for you, it's me. I understand these things."

Nina knew her cheeks were red, but she didn't say a word either in defense of herself or protest to John when he slowly released her.

Carter scratched the back of his head. "I nearly lost it with Jessica, just about a year ago, not far from where you stand." He paused, looking from Nina's face to John's. "I think the ducks were less embarrassed then than you two are now."

Nina took a deep, faintly shuddering breath. "You should have called from way back on the path."

"I did."

"Oh."

John had his hands on his hips. "You should have called a second time."

"I did. But, hey, now that you're awake and aware, I'll just be moving along." He gave them a grin and started off. "Catch you later."

He'd gone a good ten yard when Nina called, "Carter, is Jessica pregnant?"

He stopped in his tracks and turned, wearing a guarded look. "Where did you hear that?"

"Is it true?"

Taking a deep breath that straightened his back and expanded his chest beneath the blazer and shirt he was wearing, Carter allowed himself a slow smile. "Yeah, it's true. She miscarried in January, so we've been cautious about saying anything. But she's almost into her fourth month. Things look good this time."

Forgetting her embarrassment, Nina burst into a grin. "Hey, that's great. I knew she wanted a baby."

"We both do."

"How's she feeling?" John asked.

Carter shimmied a hand. "Sometimes nauseous, sometimes not. The doctor says the sickness is a sign that the baby's really settling in, which is good news after the first one. We're keeping our fingers crossed."

"I'll keep mine crossed, too," Nina said.

John put a thumb up and said in a very male way, "Good goin', Carter."

Carter tossed him a macho smile before turning and continuing along the path.

Watching him go, Nina murmured under her breath, "Are you going to say, 'I told you so'?"

"Of course not. The important thing is that it's true."

"Mmm. She did tell me she wanted a baby. I'm excited for her."

"Excited about the baby?"

"Excited because she's getting what she wants. I don't know enough about babies to get excited about them."

"Don't have any friends with kids?"

"A few. But I've never been terribly involved. I'm too busy with work. My friends seem to know that. When they meet me for lunch, it's without the kids." She allowed herself a glance at John. "Which is another reason why you and I are no good. You have a kid. I wouldn't know what in the devil to do with one."

John didn't say anything. He stood there, looking down at her, looking *into* her, seemingly, for something she was sure wasn't there. Looking back at him, all she could see was the random brush of his hair on his brow, the lean contour of his jaw, the straight slash of his nose, the tightness of his lips. It was a face that drew her even when she told herself that it shouldn't.

Finally he raised his head and looked away. "We'd better get going."

Nodding, she started off toward the duck pond, but the glow that had earlier been on the day was gone. In its place was a tension that began in the body and ended in the mind, causing an awkwardness that was underwritten with need.

They walked through the condominium that was to be the model, then through two others. Nina pointed out various features and options, just as she might have if John had been an interested buyer. They avoided looking at each other, avoided standing too close, but that didn't ease the wire that seemed strung taut between them. Whatever the distance, it hummed.

By the time they returned to the mansion, Nina was feeling strung out, herself. She was only too glad to put together a hasty goodbye to John, climb into her car and drive off. She wasn't used to confusion. Hitherto in her life, she had been the sole master of her fate. Now, though, it seemed she was losing control, if not of her fate, then of *something*.

She wished she knew what that something was.

She wished she could stop it from slipping away.

She wished she didn't feel hot, then cold, light, then dark, good, then bad.

Mostly she wished she understood what she was feeling for John. He wasn't like any man she'd ever known. He was maddeningly laid-back, but she respected him. He saw the world differently from her, but she trusted him. She liked him, but she didn't.

And she wanted him. Wanted him. He haunted her for the rest of the day and all that night. She lay in bed wide awake, remembering how he'd kissed her and held her, how safe she'd felt, how valued, how hot and needy. The need returned, making her flop one way then the next, but no position was better for the aching within. *I lie in bed imagining*, he'd said, and she imagined him imagining. She also imagined him hard, and the fever built.

She slept for an hour, then awoke, slept for another, awoke again. When her skin grew damp in the warmth of the night, she sponged herself off, but no sooner did she return to bed than she was sweaty again.

By dawn, she was fit to be tied. No man, *no man*, she vowed, could do this to her. No man was worth it. She had her life, and it was free and independent, just as she wanted. Once she had her own agency, that independence would increase. She was well on her way to where she wanted to be. She didn't need any man, *any man*.

Then, at eight o'clock, her doorbell rang. Sticky, tired and more than a little cranky, she plodded down the stairs. "Who is it?" she yelled through the wood.

"John," he called back.

Moaning softly, she put her forehead to the worn pine. It was cool, with a faint musty scent that took her out of time and place, but the relief was short-lived. John was on the other side. She didn't know what to do.

His voice came more quietly, as though he'd moved closer. "Open the door, Nina. We need to talk."

"I don't think," she said, squeezing her eyes shut, "that this is the best time."

He didn't answer. Had he been another man, she might have wondered if he'd left. But this was John.

After a minute, he spoke again, still quiet, still close. "Nina? Open the door, Nina. Please?"

She might have had a comeback had it not been for his tone of voice. Not even the thickness of the door could muffle the quiet command. But there was something else there, something even more potent. Beneath the quiet command was a hint of pleading.

Fearing she was making a huge mistake but helpless to avoid it, she gave a tiny sound of frustration, took a small step back and opened the door a crack.

6

JOHN PUSHED THE DOOR open only enough to slip through. Watching him from the corner by the hinge, Nina felt beset by every one of the wild imaginings she'd tried to stifle through the night. The fact that he wore a T-shirt and shorts didn't help any. The sight of leanly muscled legs spattered with warm brown hair stirred the fire inside her to a greater head.

"I brought donuts," he said quietly, but his eyes hadn't risen above her neck.

She was in the short nightie that she'd put on in the wee hours, and wore nothing beneath it. "I was in bed," she said, feeling the need to explain. She wouldn't normally have answered the door dressed that way. But she felt reckless, at the end of her tether. "It was a bad night."

At that, he did raise his eyes. He'd left his glasses at home, and it struck her that he looked every bit as sweaty as she felt. His hair was damp and disheveled, his skin moist. "I ran." His eyes were intent, the deepest, richest amber she'd ever seen. "I thought we could talk."

"I don't know if I can." Her need was written all over her face, she knew, but she couldn't erase it.

John seemed to see it, consider it, fight it—with about as much success as she had. After an eternity of searing silence, he muttered, "I don't want these." Dropping the bag of donuts onto the stair, he reached for her.

Coming up against his body, winding her arms around his neck, feeling him lift her nearly off her feet, Nina felt the first relief she'd had in hours. She sighed his name and held tighter, burying her face against his neck.

For the longest time, they stood like that, holding each other tighter, then tighter still, making no sounds but those of quickened breathing and the occasional whimper or moan. Nina might have stayed that way forever if it wasn't for the gradual awakening of her body to the one molding it. She began to move against him in small ways to better feel him, and when that wasn't enough, she started to use her hands.

John's own hands made slow sweeps of discovery over her back. She could tell the instant he knew for sure she was bare under her nightie by the sharp catch of his breath. Fingers splayed, his hands stole up the back of her thighs to her bottom.

"Tell me to stop if you don't want this," he said in a gravelly voice she'd never heard before. It was laced with raw need and was a stimulant in itself.

"I want it," she breathed frantically. Exploring the lean line of his hips, she pushed her fingers over his thighs. The hair there abraded her palms delightfully. "I need it," she confessed just as frantically, then let out a cry when he touched the fire between her legs. "Help me," she begged, and to convince him, she worked her fingers up under his shorts. He wore cotton briefs, but they were stretched taut.

Clearly he didn't need any convincing.

Before she had any inkling of what he was doing, he slid his hands under her thighs and lifted her. When her legs were cinched around his hips, he covered her mouth with his and devoured it whole as he started up the stairs. He didn't stop until he was in her bedroom, where he lowered her to the rumpled sheets and crouched over her.

His voice a rough burr, he drew up her nightie. "I haven't been with anyone since my wife. Do I need a condom?"

Nina helped him pull the thin fabric over her head. As soon as one hand was freed, she reached for him. "It's been longer than that for me," she whispered hurriedly as she tugged at his shirt. It was over his head in an instant, revealing a chest that was well formed and tapering. A wide wedge of hair narrowed, arrowlike, toward his fly. She reached there and touched him. "No condom."

John lowered his zipper and shifted to thrust both shorts and briefs aside. "Babies?"

"I take pills," she gasped, then, "Hurry, John, hurry." His large hand swept her under him, and no sooner did she open her legs when, like a heat seeker, he was in. Stunned by the force of his impaling, she cried out and arched up.

"Nina—"

"No, no, it doesn't hurt, it feels good, so good."

But that penetration, that first feel of his masculine strength, was only the beginning. What he proceeded to do then nearly blew her mind. He stroked her inside and out, using his hands, his mouth, his sex. He nipped, he laved. He quickened the pace and the force when her breath came more quickly. At times his movements were rhythmic, at times less so. At times he filled her to the utmost, withdrew nearly all the way, then reentered with a sharp pulsing burst that she might have feared was climactic if he hadn't continued right on again.

Hungry for everything he gave her, she touched him wherever she could, but the heat he stoked in her soon drove everything from her mind except the release coming on. She erupted with a vengeance, throbbing against him for what seemed an eternity. Lost on the other side of rapture, she wasn't able to separate her climax from his until she finally returned to consciousness enough to feel the last of the spasms shaking his body.

Slowly, breathing hard, he lowered himself over her. After a long minute, he rolled to his side and drew her along, still inside her.

She looked into his eyes, and for a minute she couldn't speak. Something caught at her throat, something deep and emotional, something she couldn't—didn't want to—understand. Making love with John had been the experience of a lifetime.

As the minutes passed and she regained her poise, she let a smile soften her lip. "Who'd have guessed it?" she finally whispered.

His brow creased in a frown that was here and gone. "Guessed what?"

"That slow, quiet, thoughtful John Sawyer was a crackerjack of unleashed virility in bed."

His cheeks were already flushed, but she could have sworn they grew more so. "I was inspired."

"You certainly were." Her smile faded. She touched his face. "That was special."

He gave a slow, thoughtful nod. "Are you sure I didn't hurt you?"

"Do I look hurt?"

He shook his head. Slowly. "You look well loved." He touched her lips, which were still warm and swollen, then her cheek, then her hair. "How can hair that is shorter than mine be feminine?"

"It's not real hard to have hair shorter than yours," she quipped, and buried her fingers in the thickness at his nape, "but I like it."

"You didn't at first."

"I didn't like much about you at first. You were slowing me down."

"I still am. It's become my cause."

She assumed he was teasing and teased him right back. "It won't work."

"Sure, it will. You're not rushing off to work right now, are you?"

She shook her head. "I don't have to be in until ten."

"If you had to be in at nine, would you be rushing?"

"Maybe." She grinned. "I suppose it would depend on how forceful that *thing* you're anchoring me here with is. Doesn't feel too forceful right now."

He grinned back. "Give it a minute."

"You think so?"

"I know so."

She waited a minute, during which time she touched his chest, tracing the hair there, teasing his nipples. "Hmm," she said, clamping her thigh higher around his when she felt him growing inside her, "I think you may be right."

"Of course I'm right." He caught her mouth and ate at it gently, then less gently as his hunger grew. Fluidly he rolled to his back, bringing her up to straddle him. His eyes were focused on her breasts, which were warm and rose tipped. After guiding her hips for a deeper joining, he left her to her own devices there and touched her breasts.

Nina watched the long fingers she admired curved around her flesh. She watched them trace her shape and weigh her fullness. She watched them knead, then rub her nipples into hard beads, then draw her forward to meet his mouth. The sight of his tongue dabbing the tip of her breast with moisture that his finger then spread, was nearly her undoing. Closing her eyes, she began to move on him, shifting forward, then back and around, feeling him grow and grow inside her until he was rising to meet her thrusts.

He brought her to a first climax by tugging her nipples into elongated points. He brought her to a second one by finding the hard bud between her legs and stroking it to fruition. He brought her to a third one by rolling her over and plunging into her with the kind of savagery she'd never have expected from him, but which drove her wild. By the time he'd emptied himself into her, their bodies were slick and spent.

For a short time, they lay limp and quiet, and at first, Nina enjoyed the closeness. Then her mind clicked on. Slowly picking up speed, it ran her through what had happened, painting pictures of what it meant, and she grew frightened. She had enjoyed herself too much, far too much. John Sawyer as a lover could be habit-forming. But she didn't have room in her life for a relationship. She didn't have time for a man like John. She had places to go. She couldn't be tied down, *wouldn't* be tied down, not even by her own desires.

"Gotta get up," she murmured from against his chest.

His arm tightened around her. "No, stay."

"Gotta get to work."

"Call in. Get someone to cover."

"I can't."

"I have a sitter till noon."

A sitter. The word represented one of the major differences between Nina and John. Flattening a firm hand on his chest, Nina ignored the lure of damp, warmly furred male flesh and levered herself up. Seconds later, she was out of bed, headed for the bathroom.

"Nina?" John called.

"I have to shower," she called back.

"Put it off."

"I can't."

She turned on the water. As soon as steam rose from it, she stepped under and began to soap herself. She worked methodically, the same way she always did. If certain spots were more sensitive than usual, even tender, she ignored that. She went on to her hair, scrubbing it hard, then rinsed, turned off the water, reached for the towel and began to rub herself dry. By the time she returned to the bedroom, John was propped up against the brass headboard, looking extraordinarily masculine against her bright pink sheets. Everything in the room was bright pink for that matter; still he didn't look foolish. Just masculine.

Ignoring that, too, she took underwear from a drawer and put it on, then a pair of silk walking shorts and a matching silk blouse, both in fuchsia. After hooking a pair of turquoise spangles onto her ears, a matching necklace around her neck and a belt around her waist, she stepped into strappy sandals. Then she shook her head, vigorously, peered into the mirror over the dresser and finger-combed her hair.

"Nina."

She looked over at John in surprise. She hadn't forgotten he was there—no way could she do that—but he'd been so still for so long that his voice, strangely sharp, startled her.

"Is that it?" he asked. His face was expressionless, his eyes level.

"What?"

"We make love, you get up and leave?"

Opening her makeup case, she began to smooth moisturizer onto her face. "I have to work."

"I want to talk."

Eyes on her own reflection, she shook her head. "Can't do that now. Maybe another time."

"When?"

She shrugged. "I don't know. I'll have to see when I'm free."

"You can be free any time you want to."

"I cannot. I have clients to service."

"So what about me?"

Her voice was low, her fingertips busy dabbing eye shadow onto her lids. "Seems to me I just serviced you."

John swore. Kicking back the sheet, he rolled to his feet and came to stand over her. Looking in the mirror, Nina caught sight of his nakedness for an instant before her own body blotted out the image, and not a moment too soon. Naked, he was stunning.

"Don't use that word with regard to what we did."

She forced a shrug, hinting at a nonchalance she didn't feel, and went on with her makeup.

"Damn it, Nina, didn't that *mean* anything to you? I mean, you're the very first woman I've been with— wanted to be with—since the debacle of my marriage, and you say that you haven't been with any other man, yet you can just climb out of bed, get dressed and move on?"

"I have work to do," she said quietly. "I take it seriously."

He rubbed a hand along the back of his neck. She could see that much. Even barefoot, he stood tall over her. Warily, with half an eye, she watched him, waiting for him to move or speak. With the other half, she finished her makeup. He hadn't said anything by the time she snapped her blusher shut and zipped it back into the bag, but he was giving her a baleful stare.

"Okay," she said, turning to him in concession, "so I'm a cold, hard bitch who's in a rush to get back to work. You can think it. You can *say* it. You knew it before this ever happened."

"Didn't this mean anything?"

"Of *course* it did. I told you, I don't play around, and I *haven't* been with a man in years. But just because we made love doesn't change anything. You still have your priorities, and I have mine. Neither of us is going to change. You knew that, John. We both knew it. That's why doing this was so stupid."

"So why did we?"

She tried to find a sensible answer, but the only thing she could come up with was, "Because we couldn't *not* do it. There's something chemical between us. It was building up and building up. This was inevitable." She turned away to reach for the purse that matched her outfit. "Dumb, but inevitable."

He stuck his hands on his lean hips, totally unselfconscious, seemingly unaware of the magnificent picture he made. "And you're sorry we did it?"

She hung her head and fingered the purse. "No. I enjoyed it."

"But you'll just turn and walk away from it?"

Her eyes shot to his. "What would you have me do?"

"Stay here. Talk to me."

"There's no *point*. What's done is done. Now I'm getting back to my life."

"You work too hard."

She made for the door. "What else is new?"

"You looked awful when I walked in here," he said, following her through the apartment.

"That was because of you. I didn't sleep last night. I kept thinking of *you*." As indictments went, it was a revealing one, but her step didn't falter.

"And you think you can stop now?"

"I'm sure as hell going to try."

"How?"

"By *working*." She reached the head of the stairs, and without a pause, started down.

"You won't be able to," he called from the top.

"Yes, I will."

"What we've done just now will haunt you."

"I won't let it."

"You can't even *look* at me!" he shouted.

Nina hadn't ever heard him shout before. The sound shook her from the top of her head to the tips of her toes, but it wasn't enough to make her turn. Lest she be stopped cold like Lot's wife, she hauled open the door and fled without a single glance back.

NINA WAS DETERMINED to do just what she'd said, to get back to work as though nothing as earth-shattering as making love with John had ever happened. Neither John nor his gorgeous body nor his masterful way of loving was going to sidetrack her from her goals of making money, making a name and making a fully independent way of life for herself.

So she poured herself into work more single-mindedly than ever that Saturday. It wasn't until after nine that night that she returned to her apartment, and she was off at seven the next morning to drive to Hartford for a one-day seminar. She was exhausted by the time she returned, feeling hot and sweaty and achy, just as she had on Friday night. Knowing John was the culprit and determined to push him from her mind, she refused to answer the phone—which rang repeatedly through the evening—and instead set herself up with a particularly tricky and, therefore, demanding book of figures relating to home mortgage options, shifting interest rates and tax plans. She worked at it until two in the morning, when a combination of exhaustion and an upset stomach got to her. Fortunately, exhaustion was the stronger of the two. She was asleep soon after her head hit the pillow.

At nine the next morning, Lee popped into her office. "Been here long?" she asked.

Nina looked up from the papers she'd been poring through. "Since eight. I'm off to show 93 Shady Hill in a couple of minutes."

Lee came closer to the desk. "You sound funny."

"Funny?"

"Tired. You look it, too. Pale."

Nina put down her pen. "I think it's a stomach bug or something. Don't come too close." Though she'd tossed the warning off half in jest, Lee backed up to the door.

"Whatever you have, I don't want. I'm making dinner Friday night at Tom's place for us and three other couples."

Nina lowered her head but not her eyes. "You're what?"

"Three other couples, and I know you're going to say that I'm crazy," she rushed on, "but I want to do it, Nina. Tom didn't ask me to. I offered."

"But he's left you sitting home alone for the past two weekends while he's off playing in New York—"

"Chicago, and it's business."

"Both weekends, *all* weekend?"

"Yes, and he was thinking of me. I showed you the scarf he brought me after last weekend. This weekend he sent flowers. It's not like he's off with another woman or anything." At Nina's dubious expression, she insisted, "He's not. Tom loves me."

Gently Nina said, "He loves what you do for him, and you love belonging."

"So, what's wrong with that?"

"Nothing—" She was about to add an "except" and then go on to say more, but caught herself. Much as she hated to see Lee hurt, she hated even more bad-mouthing Tom all the time. Lee was hooked on the man, so Nina was damned either way. It was a no-win situation. She *hated* no-win situations. Particularly when she was tired. "Listen," she said, forcing a smile, "maybe it'll work out. Maybe I'm all wrong, a cynic to the core." She tried to draw the last, but the draw went flat.

"You *must* be feeling lousy," Lee commented, eyeing her strangely. "We've been arguing about Tom for months, but you've never given up before."

"I'm not giving up. Just taking a breather. You'll hear from me again."

After a minute, softly, a bit worriedly, Lee said, "Are you sure it's just a bug that's getting you down?"

Nina touched the face of a pink slip that lay separate from the rest. "A bug and my mother. She's not doing well."

"Have you talked with her doctor?"

Setting her pink slip aside, she began to gather up her papers. "A few minutes ago. She seems to be having these little seizures. Her condition fluctuates."

"Maybe you should go out to see her."

The doctor had suggested the same thing. Again. "How can I go out there," Nina said, scooping the papers into a folder, "when there's so much to do here? This fluctuating could go on for a while. It's not even like she'd know I was there."

"But she's your mother—"

"And I do all I can. She's in the best possible place, totally at my expense, and I don't mind that. But in order to do it, I have to work. Bills don't get paid by flying all over the country." Setting the folder aside, she reached for her bag and stood.

"It's just Omaha."

"And I'll *get* there. Right now, things are buzzing here. The momentum is on. Business is great. As soon as there's a lull, I'll be on the first plane west." Holding a palm out she said, "I'm coming through the door. Move, or I won't be responsible for my germs."

Lee moved, and Nina was on her way.

THE GERMS LINGERED through the rest of Monday and Tuesday, alternately leaving Nina crampy, then not. By Wednesday, she acknowledged that what was ailing her didn't have much to do with John, other than to kill any thought of sex she might have had. That was why, when John showed up at her door on Wednesday night, she opened it.

Under the light of the porch, he looked furious. "I've been trying to reach you all week. Didn't you get my messages?"

Feeling guilty and sad, then angry at herself for feeling either, not to mention the heartthrobbing that the mere sight of him caused, she said, "I've been busy."

"So busy that you couldn't return a single phone call to the man you took to bed last Saturday?"

"It was the other way around. You took me to bed."

"Want to argue about who was willing?" He barely paused, something that unsettled her even more than his words. John took his time, always took his time—unless he was upset. "You look like hell."

"Thanks."

"I'm serious." His fury faded some as he studied her face, and his voice, more tentative now, touched her heart. "Are you all right?"

She swallowed. "I'm fine. Just busy."

"What you're doing isn't healthy—"

"Just for a little bit. This is the height of the season. Come next fall—"

"Next fall! You can't keep up this pace till then!"

"I've done it every other year. This one's no different, except that this time the end is in sight. If Crosslyn Rise comes through the way I want, by next summer I'll be out on my own. Then I'll have other people to do the running through the height of the season."

"If you're still alive."

"I'll be alive."

He was quiet then, looking at her, pensive in the way she'd come to find both comforting and provocative. Since she wasn't feeling up to provocative, she took advantage of comforting until he ended it by saying, "What about us?"

"What about us?"

"Can I see you?"

She shook her head. "I need some space."

"How much?"

"I don't know."

"Look, I'm not asking you to give up your work."

"You were last Saturday—"

"Because it was so nice holding you that I didn't want you to leave. But I thought about it after that, and you were right. You had previous appointments, and you hadn't known I was coming. So all I want now is to arrange a time when you *do* know I'm coming."

"John," she whined in frustration, "you don't *like* me."

"I don't *want* to like you. There's a difference."

"If you don't want to like me, what are you doing making a date with me?"

"Trying to find out why I like you, even if I don't want to. That was what I wanted to talk about in the first place on Saturday morning, before we got sidetracked."

Nina saw a complicated discussion on the horizon, but she was in no more of a mood for it than she was for a sixteen-ounce steak. Her stomach was feeling weird, which was how it had been feeling on and off for too long. She would see a doctor if she had the time, but she didn't have the time. Work came first. Everything else would have to wait.

"Can we save this for another time, John?"

"Sure, if you can tell me when."

"I don't know when. If you call tomorrow, I'll check—"

"I call and you're out, and you don't return my calls."

"I'll return your call this time," she said earnestly. She *really* wanted to go upstairs and lie down. "Better still, I'll call you." She was ready to promise almost anything to get him to leave. Feeling worse by the minute, she was using every bit of her strength not to let it show.

Apparently she succeeded, because he looked calmer. "Will you?"

She nodded. "First thing tomorrow, once I get into the office. I'll call and we'll arrange a time. Okay?"

He thought about it for a minute, then nodded. "I'll be waiting."

His eyes fell to her mouth, and for a minute she thought he was going to kiss her before he left. One part of her wanted that more than anything; his kiss was a balm, able to make her feel good. Then again, when his kiss was over and done she always felt worse, and she didn't need that now. She was feeling awful enough without any help from John.

For whatever his reasons, he took a step back, turned and slowly went down the walk to his car. Taking only distracted pleasure from his tight-hipped walk, Nina closed the door and leaned against it for a minute before making her way upstairs.

Despite the earliness of the hour, she went right to bed. She was hurting too much to do anything else. It occurred to her that maybe people were right and she did need more sleep, and though, given her druthers, she'd rather be working, she figured she'd give it a try.

SLEEP CAME SPORADICALLY. She dozed, only to awaken to a knotting in her stomach a few minutes later. After tossing and turning, she dozed again, but less than an hour later she was awake. Her stomach was feeling worse, aching almost steadily. Not one to take pills, she sipped water, then a little ginger ale, but nothing seemed to help. After a while, she slept, only to wake up this time in a sweat with the realization that the ache in her stomach had become a pain.

She began to grow frightened. She didn't have time to be sick. She couldn't *afford* to be sick. Desperately seeking an explanation for what was happening, she thought back on anything she had eaten that might have upset her, but what little she'd had in the past few days had been light and bland. Sipping more ginger ale, she lay down again, but the pain grew worse. Try as she might, no amount of rearranging of her body seemed to ease it.

She began to wish she had seen a doctor. She began to wonder if she should now. But other than her gynecologist, she didn't have one, hadn't ever needed one. Besides, it was after eleven. She couldn't be calling a doctor now. If worse came to worst, first thing in the morning she could make some calls and get a name.

That decided, she managed to sleep for a bit, only to rouse with a sharp cry as an acute pain suddenly tore through her insides. Clutching her stomach, she struggled to sit up, but she couldn't seem to catch her breath.

Fear gave way to terror. Something was very, very wrong. She didn't know what it was, didn't know what to do about it. Worse, she didn't think she would have been able to do anything if she *did* know what to do. She couldn't stand up straight. She could barely move.

Fighting panic, she picked up the phone by her bed, and with shaky fingers, punched out John's number. The phone rang twice before it was answered, but she didn't hear a voice.

"John?" she cried feebly. "Are you there, John?"

After a minute, she heard a groggy, "Nina?"

"Something's wrong," she cried in short, staggered bursts. "Awful pain. I don't know what to do."

His voice came stronger, all grogginess gone. "Where's the pain?"

"My stomach. I wanted to wait. But it's getting worse. I've never had this before."

"Is it cramps?"

"No. Pain. Sharp pain." She was bent in two trying to contain it.

"Which side?"

"I don't know. All over. No, more on the right."

He spoke firmly, exuding a gentle command. "Listen, babe, I'm gonna run next door for a sitter—"

"It's two in the morning. You can't—"

"Can you make it down to the front door?"

"I don't know. I think so."

"I want you to go there, unlock the door and wait for me. I won't be more than ten minutes."

"Oh, God, John, I'm sorry—"

"Go downstairs and wait."

"Okay." Trembling, she hung up the phone. Then, fearful that if the pain got worse she wouldn't make it, she stumbled out of bed and headed for the door. She stopped against the doorjamb, doubled over in pain, caught her breath, then stumbled on. Reaching the stairs, she sat on the top step and, one by one, eased herself down. She barely had time to unlatch the door at the bottom before she crumpled back onto the lowest step, in excruciating pain.

She must have passed out, because the next thing she knew, John was crouching down by her side. "Nina? *Nina.*"

His hand was cool against the burning on her forehead, her cheek, her neck, but it was the worry in his voice that reached her. She forced her eyes open. "I'm okay," she said, but even her voice was far away. Her insides were on fire, hurting like hell. With an anguished moan, she closed her eyes against the pain.

"You'll be fine," John said as he lifted her. The words came through a fog, the same way as the feel of his arms did. What was happening inside her body seemed to be putting distance between herself and the world. But trust was an intuitive thing. She trusted John. For that reason, as soon as she was in his arms, as soon as she felt him start to carry her out to his car, she yielded her well-being to him and turned her own focus to fighting the intense pain that was eating her alive.

WAKEFULNESS CAME to Nina in fits and snatches over the course of the next few days. She seemed able to grasp at consciousness only briefly, enough to find out what had happened and ease the fear in her mind before yielding to the effects of anesthesia, painkillers and illness. At times when she woke up, there were doctors with her, poking and prodding, asking her questions that she had barely the strength to answer. At times there were nurses bathing her, shifting her, checking the fluid that ran from bottles, down thin tubes, into her veins.

At times John was there. Of all the faces she saw in her daze, his was the clearest. Of all the things she remembered hearing, his words were the ones that registered.

"You had a ruptured appendix," he told her during one of those first bouts with wakefulness.

"Ruptured?" she whispered, dry mouthed and groggy.

He was sitting close by the side of the bed and had her free hand in both of his, pressed to his throat. "But it's okay now. You'll be just fine."

Another time, when she awoke to find him perched on the side of the bed by her hip, she asked in a croak, "What did they do?"

He smiled crookedly. "Took out your appendix. Cleaned up the mess in there. Sewed you back up."

Moving her hand to her stomach, she felt what seemed like mountains of bandages. "So much stuff here."

"It'll come off soon. How do you feel?"

"Hot."

"That's the fever. They're giving you antibiotics. It should help pretty soon. Are your hurting?"

"A little. And tired."

Brushing her cheek with the back of his hand, he said, "Then sleep."

Given the quiet command and the warm assurance of his body close by, she did, and those hours of sleep were the best. When she awoke alone, there was an emptiness along with the pain and the heat, and she sought sleep again as an escape. Aloneness was bleak, strangely frightening. Given that she'd spent so much of her life alone, that would have mystified her if she'd been in any condition to analyze it. But she wasn't.

For nearly three days, she was in a limbo of fever and pain. Slowly, on the morning of the fourth, she began to emerge from it. The doctors were the first to visit, in the course of making their rounds. Then the nurses came in to do their thing. And then John.

She was awake this time when he appeared at the door. His face brightened when he saw that her eyes were open.

"Hey," he said, coming inside, "you're up."

"Finally." Her voice was still dry, weak and hoarse, and she was feeling more feeble than that, but the sight of him pleased her.

"You look better."

"I look awful."

"You've been up looking at yourself in the mirror?" he teased.

But she nodded. "They made me get out of bed."

"That's great," he said with enthusiasm, then grew more cautious. "How was it?"

"Terrible. I can't stand up straight."

"That'll come."

"I got dizzy. I nearly passed out, and that was just between the bed and the bathroom. It's discouraging."

"Were you expecting to get out of bed and dance a jig?"

"No, but I thought I'd be able to *walk*, at least. I mean, I've been lying here doing nothing for three full days—"

"Doing nothing?" His brows went up for an instant. When they came down, his expression was dark. "Babe, you were fighting for your life. It was touch and go for a while there. Didn't they tell you that?"

"Doctors exaggerate things."

"Not this time," John said, and his face underscored the words. "You've been really sick, Nina. They wanted to know if there were any close relatives who should be notified."

That sobered her a bit. "What did you tell them?"

"What Lee told me."

"Lee?"

"I called your office Thursday morning to let them know you wouldn't be in, and she was the one who called back. She's been in a couple of times, but you've been asleep." He settled gently on the side of the bed and said in a quiet, compassionate voice, "She told me about your mother. I'm sorry, Nina. I didn't know she was so sick."

Nina closed her eyes. "She's been sick for a long time."

"That's what Lee said."

He grew quiet, giving Nina the opportunity to go on, but she wasn't up for that. During the past few days, on those occasions when she'd woken up alone, she had thought about her mother more than she might have expected. She was feeling very strange about some of the thoughts she'd had, particularly now, knowing how sick she had been herself.

"Want to sleep?" John whispered.

She shook her head and whispered back, "I'm okay," but she didn't open her eyes.

He took her hand. "You can sleep if you want. I'll be here when you wake up."

"You've been here a lot."

"Whenever I could."

"You shouldn't have."

"This is important."

"But you have other things—"

"I have backup. Right now, this is where I want to be."

At the words, she felt a slow knot form in her throat. Turning her head away, she murmured, "I'm sorry."

"What for?"

"Being a pain in the butt. You've got more important things to do than sit here with me. You should be home with J.J."

"J.J.'s with a sitter. He's fine."

She squeezed her eyes shut. "He's with a sitter too much lately, and all because of me. First I drag you out in the middle of the night, then you feel you have to stay here—"

He touched her lips, stilling her words. "Thank God you did drag me out in the middle of the night. If you'd waited for morning, it might have been too late. And as for my staying here, I don't have to. I want to. Think of me as your warden. I'm gonna make sure you don't do too much too fast."

Her warden. She didn't know whether he was that or something else, but she did know that he was special. Lee might have stopped by to visit, but she'd left. Her other friends had sent cards and flowers, even called. But John had come. Time and again, he'd come. And stayed.

Feeling suddenly weepy, she tried to turn over onto her side, but the attempt brought a wince. John's hands were there, then, helping her, propping pillows behind her to give her support. "Okay, now?" he asked, leaning over her shoulder.

She nodded. Seconds later, she felt him brush at the tears escaping from the corners of her eyes.

"Ah, Nina," he whispered.

"I'm okay," she whispered back. "I'll just rest for a while." Taking his hand from her cheek, she tucked it inside hers, between her breasts. "Rest for just a little while," she murmured, and let herself go to sleep.

John was there when she woke up, then again later that night, then the next morning. He helped her out of bed and into the bathroom, then back into bed. He sat close beside her when she ate Jell-O, then later, custard, then later, a soft-boiled egg. He left for a little while at the end of the day but was back after he'd put J.J. to bed, then sat with her until after eleven.

By the Tuesday morning, her sixth in the hospital, she was finally feeling better. The intravenous solutions had been replaced by oral antibiotics, her stitches by tape. She was still sleeping on and off through the day, but she was beginning to think about work more and more. There was so much she wanted to do. Each day she lazed around in the hospital was another day wasted.

"When can I go home?" she asked the doctor after he checked the incision and her chart and appeared pleased with both.

"Another two or three days."

"*Two* or *three*?" That surprised her. "But I'm fine now. I'm up and around. The worst of the pain is gone, and without any medication for it." One of the first things she'd done was refuse painkillers. She hated being doped up.

"But there's still the danger of infection," the doctor pointed out. "Your body's suffered a trauma. You need to be monitored for that. And you need rest."

"I can get rest at home."

"But will you?" He was middle-aged, with a pleasant manner, a gentle sense of humor and particularly expressive eyes. Those eyes were now filled with an I-know-your-type look, for which she had only herself to blame. She had told him about her work. In the telling, some of her compulsion must have come through. "You live alone. There'll be no one to keep tabs on how much you do or don't do."

"I'm a big girl. I can keep tabs on myself."

"But will you?"

"I'll rest."

"With a pen in one hand and the phone at your ear?" he chided. "No, I'd rather you stay here a little longer."

"But there's a shortage of beds," she argued, having read that time and again in the paper.

"Not for sick people, there isn't."

"I'm not sick."

"You were. More sick than some. And it didn't help that you were run-down." He looked about to scold her for that. Instead, he simply said, "I'm not sure I can trust that you'll rest at home."

Though she was beginning to tire, Nina wasn't giving up the fight. "I'll rest better there than here. Sleeping was fine here when I was half out of it, but now I wake up with every little noise in the hall, and then you guys come at me at six in the morning—"

"You're still weak, Nina. You need watching."

A low voice came from the door. "What if I were to watch her?"

Nina turned her head to find John there, and felt a little more peaceful than she had moments before. He did that to her, had a way of making her feel safe. It had to do with his confidence, she guessed, and that air of quiet command. He would argue with the doctor. He knew how much better she was feeling.

Responding to his question, the doctor said, "Can you do that?"

"If she's at my house, I can."

His house? But that wasn't what Nina had in mind. Not at *all*. "Uh, wait a minute, John. That would be tough."

"Why so?" he asked, approaching the bed. "I have a perfectly good guest room with a perfectly good bed. You can sleep in it just as well as you can sleep in your own bed, and there wouldn't be the hospital interruptions."

There wouldn't be a telephone, either, Nina knew. Nor would she feel comfortable having people stop by from the office with updates on work. Nor would she be able to call clients. John would never stand for that.

"I could make sure you eat," he went on, "and I'd be able to see if you were worse and get you back here in time." His gaze shifted to the doctor. "Would you let her leave if she stayed with me?"

The doctor didn't have to give it a second thought. "Sure."

His easy agreement infuriated Nina. "That's ridiculous," she said, but more quietly. She was beginning to fade and was appalled by it. Before she totally lost her strength, she said to John, "What about J.J.?"

"What about him?"

"He'd see me."

John considered that. "Yes."

"But you don't want that."

"Uh, listen," the doctor interrupted, "this is sounding like a private discussion." To John, he said, "If you want her, she's yours, but not until this afternoon. I want to do a final blood workup before I discharge her. Why don't you leave word at the desk when you decide what to do. I'll be on the floor for most of the morning."

"Dr. Caine?" Nina called weakly. She wanted to go to *her* home, not John's. She didn't want to owe him a thing. And she wanted to be free to work.

"I'll be back," the doctor said from the door and disappeared.

She took in a big breath and let it slowly out, sinking deeper into the pillows as she did.

"You're feeling tired, aren't you?" John asked.

She wanted to argue, but couldn't. Silently she nodded.

"Caine says it'll be that way for a while."

She wanted to ask—indignantly—when John had spoken to Dr. Caine, but it was a foolish notion. John had brought her to the hospital on that nightmare of a night. He'd been the one to tell the doctor what she was feeling, since she was unconscious. He'd been the one in the waiting room while she was in surgery and the one in her room when she woke up. Of course, he'd spoken with the doctor. Naturally the doctor trusted him.

So did she, but going to his house involved matters beyond trust. It involved an intrusion in his life that was different from the time she'd hitherto taken up. It involved meeting J.J.

As though reading her mind, John carefully lowered himself by her side. "I've thought about this a lot, Nina. The idea of your coming home with me isn't out of the blue. If you're leaving the hospital, you need to be with someone who can take care of you."

"I can take care of myself."

"Maybe in a few days. But not now. At least, not very well. You need to rest. You don't need to be thinking about making a meal when you're hungry or answering the door when the bell rings or doing work. Work will wait," he said with subtle emphasis. "It'll wait till you're well."

In other circumstances, Nina would have argued up a blue streak about that. But either she was simply too weak to argue, or his slow, confident tone was too persuasive. So she let it go for the time being. At the moment, the issue of work didn't seem quite as important as the one of John's son.

"What about J.J.?" she asked again, very softly. "If I were to stay at your place, what would you tell him?"

"Just what I've been telling him all week, that you're a friend who's sick."

"I'll be in the way there."

He shook his head. "You're not demanding. You barely let me do things for you here. I can't imagine you turning into a spoiled witch once we leave."

"But there's J.J."

John's eyes searched her. "You seem hung up on that. He's just a child."

"Just a child? He's *your* child, and he means the world to you. You didn't want me to meet him—"

"Whoa. You said that before. What makes you think it?"

"You always get a sitter when you see me."

His lips grew wry. "Because what I'm thinking of doing when I see you isn't exactly appropriate for a child, any child, to see."

"But that Sunday when you came by my office for the brochure, you could have brought him, still you didn't. You left him with friends at the beach."

"Because he was having fun."

"If he'd started to cry when you left, would you have brought him?"

John was contemplative for a minute. "Maybe." Slowly he added, "But maybe you're right, in a way. I want to protect J.J. from hurt, so I've kept our lives— his and mine—very simple. My job is perfect for that.

I haven't brought strangers around often, and in particular, I haven't brought women. I haven't wanted to confuse him."

"If you bring me home now, he will be confused."

He thought about that. "I can explain that you're a friend."

"But I'll be there, in your house, then when I'm better, I'll be gone. Won't *that* confuse him?"

"I'll explain that you're better."

Nina wasn't expressing herself well, and the more she tried, the more frustrated she grew. Closing her eyes, she sighed. "Oh, John."

"What?" he asked with such gentleness that the words, sounding fragile and meek, spilled out.

"I'm awful with kids. I don't know what to do, and J.J.'s not just any kid. He's special. But what if I do something wrong? What if I *say* something wrong?" In the silence that followed, she dared open her eyes. John's were every bit as gentle as his voice.

"You'll be at my place to rest, not to perform," he said, and gave a sad smile. "Besides, you don't have to worry about saying the wrong thing to J.J. He won't hear you, anyway."

Feeling John's sadness, she closed her eyes. From within that cocoon of darkness, she heard his low-spoken words. "I'd like you to meet him, Nina. I'd like him to meet you. It's time."

She wasn't quite sure what that meant, but somehow it didn't seem important. If John wanted her, truly wanted her to recuperate at his home, she'd go. There was a danger in it. She would have to be careful not to compromise her own independence in any long-term way. But she was sick. And he was offering. And there was a small part of her—call it expediency or curiosity or just plain old selfishness—that wanted it, truly wanted it, too.

7

THE DOCTOR DID HIS WORKUP and was sufficiently satisfied with Nina's condition to release her into John's charge late that afternoon. Wearing the loose sundress and sandals that Lee had brought by earlier in the day, she walked slowly to the elevator, holding lightly to John's arm.

"Just your speed, eh?" she teased.

"I'm not complaining." He studied her face. "Are you okay?"

"Uh-huh." But she wished it was true. Her legs felt weak, and since she refused to walk hunched over, her incision pulled. The doctor had promised that both the weakness and the pulling would get better each day, but she was impatient. She wasn't used to being sick. The thought of being slowed down frustrated her.

Nonetheless, by the time the elevator ride was done and they had crossed the parking lot, she was grateful to sit. Easing herself gingerly into the car, she put her head back against the seat and worked at regaining her breath.

"You're pale as a ghost," John observed the instant he joined her. "Are you sure you don't want to go back in there?"

She shook her head. The *last* thing she wanted was to go back in there. She had places to go and things to do, and though she would rather be heading for her own home, given the doctor's stubbornness, John's home would have to do. At least she'd be able to sleep when *she* wanted to, then use the rest of the time to think. John might not allow her to spend hours on the phone, but she would be able to do some creative planning and write out instructions for Lee regarding Crosslyn Rise.

"I'll be fine," she said in a thin voice. "I'm just not used to being upright for so long."

"Try this." Gently he eased her down so that her head was braced in the fold of his groin. "Better?"

She sighed against his thigh. "Much."

Putting the car in gear, he started off. "You were lying this way when I drove you in last Wednesday night. Do you remember?"

"No. That whole time's a blur."

He stroked her hair. "I was scared."

"Did you guess what was wrong?"

"Uh-huh. That's why I was scared. It used to be that once an appendix ruptured, the person was gone. I figured yours had ruptured, but I didn't know when. It must have been right before you phoned me."

She shivered.

"Cold?"

He was already reaching to lower the air conditioning when she shook her head. "Just remembering. The pain was so awful. I've never felt anything like it."

"Thank goodness you knew to call me."

She thought about that, just as she'd done more than once while lying in her hospital bed. She could have called Lee. She could have called Martin. She could have called 911. But she'd called John. She hadn't seriously considered any other option. And while one part of her—the part that had built a life on the concepts of independence and self-sufficiency—resented it, she had to accept the practical fact that of all the people she knew, John had the coolest, calmest head on his shoulders.

Reaching for his hand, she tucked it under her chin. "I haven't thanked you. You came. You knew what to do and did it. You saved my life."

He cleared his throat. "All we need now are a few violins—"

"I mean it, John. I'm very grateful."

"Good. Then you can show your gratitude by being a good girl over the next few days and staying in bed."

"*Staying* in bed?"

"At least at the start."

She settled in against his thigh.

After a short silence, he said, "What? No argument?"

"I'm too tired," she said in a feeble drone, answering the very question she kept asking herself. Going with John this way was against all she stood for, but the circumstances were mitigating. "I didn't realize it at the hospital. I just wanted to get out." After a minute, she said, "Now I just want to rest."

"Then rest. We'll be there soon."

She let the hum of the car and the strength of John's thigh lull her. "Get me up before we reach your street?"

"Why?"

"So your customers don't see me drag my head from your lap and think awful things."

He chuckled. "I'll get you up. But watch what you say, or you'll get me up, too. Then the customers will really have a show."

Had she been feeling well, Nina would surely have marveled that the bookish John Sawyer was into double entendres. Had she been feeling well, she would have been turned on by it. But she wasn't feeling well. Sex was the last thing on her mind. Or nearly. She couldn't resist a smile at the image of the proper bookseller, improperly aroused, escorting her across the front lawn.

In no time it seemed, John was nudging her awake. "Rise and shine," he whispered, and helped her sit up as he turned onto his street. Seconds later, he turned into his driveway and pulled directly up to the side door. Though Nina guessed that he normally parked by the garage that stood well behind the house, she didn't argue. Walking through the hospital had exhausted her. She was still feeling the drain.

With John's help, she eased herself from the vehicle. As they walked toward the door, her heartbeat quickened. She wanted to attribute it to the weakness of her limbs, and that might in part have been true. But she was also nervous.

"What will he be doing now?" she asked in a whisper. "Does he watch TV?"

John didn't have to ask who she was talking about. "Sometimes. But I think he's out." He pulled the door open.

"Out?"

"With the girls."

"Oh." She was relieved, then again, disappointed. Starting up the stairs with John's arm in light possession of her waist, she said, "I'm beginning to think he's a phantom. He's never around when I expect him to be."

"He'll be back," John said with certainty, and tightened his arm when she seemed to lag. "Maybe these stairs weren't such a good idea," he muttered.

"I'd have had stairs at my place, too," she said, huffing more with each step. "Once I get to the top, I'll be fine."

"Once you lie down you'll be fine."

She agreed with him there. With little more than a vague impression of lots of browns and blues, she let him guide her past the living room and down a hall to the very last room. It too was blue, blue and white, not quite masculine, not quite feminine, not quite decorated, but simple and sweet. The one thing that interested her most though was the bed. It was a double, had two fluffy pillows and was covered with a quilt that had already been turned back. Desperate to lie down, she crossed to it, sat on its edge and, bracing her stomach with an arm, carefully lowered her head to the pillow. John lifted her feet behind her.

She sighed and close closed her eyes. "Ah, that's better."

"You're sweating."

"I'm okay."

"Is there a nightshirt with the clothes Lee picked up?"

"Should be." She heard him take the bag from his shoulder and drop in onto a chair, then unfasten it and rummage through.

"This is pretty," he mused dryly.

She managed to lift her head and open an eye, but what she saw didn't please her. Lee had packed her skimpiest nightie. She couldn't possibly wear it, not with a little boy running around.

With a moan, she returned her head to the pillow. "I'm okay like this for now." She'd worry about nightwear later.

But John had other ideas. Without a word, he left the room, returning moments later with a shirt of his own. "Assuming this reaches your knees, it'll be loose and soft and decent," he said, and began to unbutton it.

Nina was too weak to protest when he helped her off with the sundress and on with the shirt. She managed some of the buttons while he did the others, then, while she lay down again, he rolled up the sleeves. After surveying his work and judging it acceptable, he flipped a switch on the wall. A soft whir of air drew Nina's notice to the ceiling, where a fan had gently started to turn.

"Nice," she said with a small smile, but what was nicer was the clean way she felt in John's shirt, the way the mattress molded to her body as the hospital one had never done, the freshness of the linen by her cheek. "I think I'll just rest awhile now," she murmured and, within minutes, dozed off.

WHEN SHE AWOKE, she was disoriented. At first she thought she was at the hospital, but the smell wasn't right, too pleasant, not antiseptic at all. Then she thought she was at home, but the sound wasn't right, too smooth, almost a hum, like the fan she had always wanted but didn't yet have. Then she remembered where she was and slowly opened her eyes.

Before her, standing nearly at eye level little more than an arm's length away, was J.J. Sawyer. He had thick shiny hair that was a shade lighter in color than his father's dark brown and fell over his forehead in full bangs, skin that was smooth and gently tanned, a small nose and serious mouth. Barefoot, he was wearing a faded T-shirt over denim shorts. His limbs were slender though not skinny. In fact, while she had expected him to look frail, that wasn't the case. Had it not been for the thick glasses he wore and the hearing aids on each ear, he'd have looked like anyone's rough-and-tumble, normal healthy four-year-old son.

Feeling an unexpected tug at her heartstrings, Nina smiled. "Hi," she said. She didn't move other than to lift a hand and flex it in a small wave.

He waved back, but, with the movement of her hand, his attention had been drawn to her wrist. She followed the line of his gaze to the identification band the hospital had put there. She hadn't thought to take it off. Holding her arm out, she let J.J. take a closer look.

He turned the band slowly, first one way, then the next.

Had she been able, Nina would have slipped it off and given it to him, but by design it was too small to slip off. Shooting for second best, she mimed cutting through the band with scissors. She pointed to him, then to the door, then repeated the cutting motion.

J.J.'s eyes, magnified by the glasses, rose to hers. She raised her brows in invitation, smiled, nodded and made the cutting motion again. Without a sound, he turned and scampered from the room.

Only then aware of the quickening of her pulse, Nina took a deep, steadying breath. Either she'd gotten her point across, or she'd sent J.J. off to his father with reports of a real weirdo in the spare room. But, what the hell, how was she supposed to know what a four-year-old did? All kids used scissors, didn't they? Or was it only ones older than four? She tried to remember what *she'd* been doing at that age, then decided against it. Nothing about her childhood had been normal.

Before she could give it another thought, J.J. ran back into the room, carrying a pair of small, blunt-tipped scissors. Feeling victorious that she had made herself understood, Nina held out her wrist. "Can you do it?" she asked, pointing from him to the bank, to the scissors and back.

Opening the scissors, he slipped them under the band and tried to cut, but the plastic resisted the dull blades.

"Try again," Nina coaxed. Giving him a thumbs-up sign in encouragement, she pushed the band deeper into the jaws of the scissors. He made another single slash with the scissors, but to no avail. His brows came down, his small mouth thinned.

Feeling his frustration, Nina held up a finger to tell him to wait, then pushed the band even deeper into the scissors and made a series of repeated movements with her fingers. He took the hint. Using smaller cuts, he finally managed to pierce the plastic. Once that initial piercing was done, the split grew longer with each cut.

Though he was the one making the effort, Nina was the one who had worked herself into a cold sweat of determination by the time the scissors finally made it all the way through. "Good boy!" she said with a grin.

J.J., too, was grinning when he looked up at her.

"Thank you," she mouthed, and his grin widened, then his eyes followed suit when she offered him the band. "It's yours if you want it. You earned it."

He couldn't have heard her words, wasn't even looking at her face at the moment she said them, so he couldn't possibly have read her lips, but the excitement she saw in his eyes was an eloquent as could be.

Nudging the band into his hand, she nodded. He took it, turned and ran from the room.

Again Nina felt the race of her heart and concentrated on slowing down. J.J. had done the work, but she was exhausted. Pathetic as it was, it was a fact of life, for this day at least. If she rested today, surely she'd feel stronger tomorrow.

But she had barely closed her eyes when the patter of small running feet returned. J.J was back, one hand holding her band, the other closed into a fist. Squatting down by the side of the bed, he put the band between his feet, opened his fist, rearranged its contents, then stood and offered her the five jelly beans that lay carefully cupped inside.

Nina hadn't eaten much in the past week. Her stomach was just getting back to normal. Sweaty jelly beans weren't the kind of food that the doctor would have necessarily recommended. But she grinned at J.J., put on an honored look and, one by one, telling him how good each was with the roll of her eyes, ate the beans.

"Dee-licious," she said with a final eye roll. Then she settled into a smile and gave him a silent but exaggerated, "Thank you."

With a grin, he retrieved the band from where it had been safely resting and ran from the room again. She half expected him to be back seconds later with something else, but he wasn't, and it was just as well. She was feeling tired again.

Gingerly rolling over, she pulled the sheet up to her chest, closed her eyes and slept. This time when she awoke, the room was bathed in the early-evening sun and the eyes she looked into were John's.

"Hi, there," he said. He was sitting on the side of the bed. She wondered how long he'd been there.

"Hi."

"Sleep well?"

"Mmm-hmm."

"Feeling better?"

"For now." Wryly she added, "In five minutes, I'll be tired again."

"That'll pass."

"I hope so."

"Are you hungry?"

"No. I had a snack last time I was up. Five jelly beans."

"So I was told."

"He's sweet, John. So sweet."

"I think so."

"Does he look like his mom?" Other than the hair, she didn't see the resemblance to John, though that could well have been due to the discrepancy in size and age.

John thought about it for a minute, finally saying, "It's hard for me to tell. When I see J.J., I see J.J. He has a way about him that's all his own, maybe because of the problems, I don't know. But I've never done much comparing of him either to other children or to adults."

"He's bright and quick. He knew just what I was saying."

"About the bracelet?"

"He told you?"

"Showed me. Made me tape it together so he could wear it." His eyes rose and went past her. "Speak of the devil." He gestured with his hand and spoke with the same kind of exaggerated mouth movements that Nina had used. "Come on in."

Too content lying where she was to turn, Nina asked, "How good is he at that?"

"At lipreading? He gets short things, simple things, far more than a normal four-year-old would get but far less than he will in a year or two or three." Scooping the boy onto his lap, he said, "J.J., this is Nina." Then he snickered. "It'd help, of course, if he were looking at my lips, but he's too busy looking at you. Not that I blame him," he added under his breath.

Nina gave the child the same kind of small wave that she'd given him before. With his smaller hand—circled now with the taped plastic band—he returned it. Then she looked at his mouth, which was surrounded by a faint orange ring. "Is that spaghetti sauce I see?" She ran her finger around her lips.

Carefully, J.J. put the tips of his baby fingers together and drew them apart with the faintest of spiraling motions. John made a different motion, bringing one hand down from his mouth, palm up, into the other. Tipping his head back, J.J. gave him a grin.

For Nina's benefit, John explained. "He signed 'spaghetti.'" He repeated the motion J.J. had made, doing it more neatly so that she could see. "I praised him back in sign."

Nina was impressed. "Does he sign a lot?"

"About as much as he reads lips. We work on both with the therapists, and I reinforce it at home. Spaghetti's one of his favorite things. He eats it a lot, so he has the sign down pat." He paused, leaned over, planted a kiss on his son's forehead. "Overall, he does damn well at it, for a four-year-old."

Nina felt a touch of envy for the love passing from father to son. Then she thought of something else and felt a shaft of timidity. "Does he get frustrated with people who don't sign?"

"He gets frustrated when he wants something and can't make himself known, but every kid does that. As far as signing goes, he only gets frustrated when someone who doesn't sign gets frustrated with him."

"Do his sitters sign?"

"A little. The girls do it more than the grown-ups. They think it's a game." Snorting, he nuzzled the top of J.J.'s head. "They wouldn't think it was such fun if it was their only means of communication." Leaning sideways, he signed something to J.J., who promptly nodded. In the next instant, John lowered him to the floor and stood. "He's going to help me bring in your supper."

Nina pushed herself up on an elbow. "John, I can go into the kitchen."

"Not tonight."

"I can do it," she insisted. With her mind clear and her body newly rested, she was uncomfortable in the role of the helpless patient.

"Why should you try, when I can bring it in here?"

"Because you shouldn't be waiting on me."

"Yes, I should. That was the whole point in your coming here. It was the only condition the doctor let you out."

"But I don't want—"

"Tough," he cut in with uncharacteristic sharpness. "It's done." Following J.J.'s lead, he left the room.

Nina didn't resume the fight when he returned with a dinner tray. She only made it through half of the spaghetti and sauce he'd given her, and even less of the salad, before she felt too tired to go on. "I'll have more later," she said, putting her head onto the pillow as soon as he removed the tray. To her chagrin, she fell asleep.

She awoke once not long after that to find J.J. in pajamas, playing on the floor with a brightly colored plastic tow truck and two matching cars. His small head, hair clean and damp, was bent in concentration, and from time to time a low, flat sound came from his throat, clearly an imitation of the truck's roar. She wondered if he ever heard the real thing, or simply felt the vibrations. She wondered if he heard anything at all. He wasn't wearing his hearing aids. She wondered what a totally silent world might be like.

Loath to disturb him, she simply watched for a short time until her eyes felt heavy again. Then, bidding him a silent good-night, she went back to sleep.

WHEN SHE AWOKE AT ELEVEN, John was sitting in the nearby chair, reading a book. After seeing her to the bathroom and back, he made her a frothy milk shake that she was sure he'd slipped an egg or two into, but she didn't complain. It was cool and tasty, smooth going down. Feeling comfortably full, she went back to sleep.

WHEN SHE AWOKE the next morning, J.J. was on the floor again, this time perched on his heels, reading a book of his own. From what Nina could see, it contained far more pictures than words, but he turned the pages in order and seemed engrossed in what he saw.

She rolled over and stretched, but he couldn't hear the rustle of the sheets. So she ruffled his hair. At that he looked up. Seeing her awake, he jumped up and, leaving the book on the floor, ran for John.

She was sitting on the edge of the bed when he arrived. "Did you have him standing guard?" she teased.

The only answer she got was a shrug. His gaze was fixed on her face. "How did you sleep?"

"Soundly. It's peaceful here."

He continued to study her, finally deciding, "You look better."

"It's about time."

"Want some breakfast?"

For the first time since she'd taken sick, she said. "Just a little." But "just a little," as interpreted by John, turned out to be nearly as large a breakfast as Ronnie's Special at the Easy Over. She came nowhere near finishing. "You're trying to fatten me up," she complained. "Much more of this and my clothes won't fit."

"You're clothes don't fit now. You've lost weight."

She guessed it was true, though her stomach still felt puffy near the incision. "Maybe I could get dressed today and see."

But John shook his head. "Tomorrow."

Figuring that he was taking his orders from the doctor, she didn't argue. But she wasn't beyond bargaining a little. "How about the newspaper, then? I haven't seen one in a week."

He considered that for a minute, then used the tip of his sneaker to gently nudge J.J., who had returned to his book. A brief sign sent the boy scurrying off.

Nina repeated the sign, a double snapping of the heels of her hands with her fingers aimed in opposite directions. "Newspaper?"

"That's right."

She filed the information. "How do you say 'thank you'?"

John mouthed the words.

"In sign," she prompted dryly, and repeated the sign when he showed it to her, then used it when J.J. ran back in, the proud bearer of the morning paper.

Unfortunately, she wasn't as proud of herself when, barely halfway through the paper, she set it aside, slid down on the pillows and fell back to sleep.

THE PATTERN REPEATED ITSELF through all of Wednesday. She woke up feeling bright eyed, only to wither after a brief time. Fighting it seemed to do no good. Her body had a will of its own.

"Is this normal?" she asked John later that day. Back in bed, feeling as though she'd run a marathon rather than just taken a shower, she was discouraged.

"Perfectly normal," he said, flanking her hips with his hands.

"But I wasn't this tired in the hospital."

"You were, but you didn't think anything of it. Here, you keep thinking you should be up and around."

"I should be."

He shook his head in the slow way that was an answer in itself.

"I should be," she insisted. "When I stop to think about the work I'm missing—"

"Lee is covering for you."

"I know, but I should be doing it."

He pulled back a little, and his look grew dark. "That's exactly the kind of argument that nearly got you killed. If it hadn't been for your compulsion to work, you'd have seen a doctor earlier and gotten by with a simple appendectomy. Instead, you let it go, so you ended up going through ten times more danger and pain. Stick inconvenience in there wherever you want. If you're missing work, it's your own fault."

"But what about Crosslyn Rise?" she asked more meekly. She always felt bad when John raised his voice or spoke more quickly than usual, which was what he was doing then. "We've come so far with it, and it's almost there. If we're launching the marketing program with an open house on the Fourth—"

"That's barely two weeks off, Nina," he interrupted more calmly but with no less force. "You can't hold it then. Put it off a month."

"A *month*!"

He gave a slow nod. "Carter and Jessica have no problem with that."

"You talked with them about my work?" Not wanting to sound annoyed after all he'd done, she spoke with care, but John must have sensed some of what she was thinking, because he came back firmly.

"It's my work, too, and Carter's and Jessica's, and of course I talked to them. They've been worried about you. You're part of the team."

"Part of the team, that's right, and I have no intention of letting down on my end. I can plan the open house, John. Right from this bed I can plan it. Assuming Christine gets the finishing touches done on the model condo, I can handle it. There's nothing much to putting a few ads in the paper, sending around a few invitations, making a few phone calls to get interest humming."

John turned sideways, looking back at her over a shoulder. "And what about standing on your feet for hours on end talking with lookers, not to mention giving tours of the grounds?"

"I can have other people do that."

"Wait a month."

"But the Fourth is a perfect weekend."

"People go away on the Fourth. Wait a month."

"People go away in *August*."

"So wait until Labor Day."

"Impossible."

"Then the last week in July."

"How about the weekend after the Fourth?"

"The last week."

"The next to last week." Wrapping her arms around her middle, she slid lower into the sheets. "And that's as much as I'll give."

Silently he stared straight ahead while she studied his profile, trying to guess at his mood. She knew she irked him at times, particularly when it came to work, but she didn't want him angry.

Anger wasn't what she saw when he turned his head, but rather a trace of amusement. "I'm surprised you gave that much," he mused. "I expected more of a fight."

In another day and age, she might have said something clever, clicked her heels and walked out of the room, but she wasn't up to any of that. "Believe it or not," she said with a sigh, "I don't love fighting even when I *do* feel good."

"Which you don't right now."

"Weak, just weak. Damn it."

Taking a deep breath, John straightened his arms on either side of her again. Looking deeply into her eyes, he said with exquisite gentleness, "Is it so awful to be weak once in a while?"

"I *hate* being weak," she ground out, feeling that hatred in her very marrow.

"But once in a while? Not all the time, just once in a while?"

Nina shut her eyes against the flood of memories that his words brought back. *Once in a while, that's all, I'll just see him once in a while. I can't not see him at all. He's too good to me for that. I need him, Nina. I do.*

"Nina?"

Feeling a great wave of sadness, she opened her eyes to John. At first she didn't think she had the strength to answer. Then she saw the concern—and question—in his eyes and knew that, given all he'd done for her, the least she could do was to tell him the truth.

Quietly, soberly, almost fraily, she said, "My mother used to ask me that, whether it was wrong to be weak once in a while. Her weakness was men. She loved being held by them and kept by them. She didn't demand anything except that they give her enough to get by, and for years, that's what she did. She got by. She got *us* by. We never had anything extra, and that was okay by me, except that she was never around, and that *wasn't* okay, because I wanted her. When I was old enough to ask her to get a real job with regular hours, she said she couldn't. So-and-so was too good to her. She couldn't give him up. We used to fight about it, more when I got older and the so-and-sos kept changing. I'd tell her she was weak, and she'd say that was okay. Then I started seeing the bruises, and I'd tell her she didn't have to stand for that, but she would. She'd take it over and over again. Then she started in with the pills—"

Nina swallowed hard and, with the motion, felt suddenly more tired than ever before. Wearily she turned her head to the side.

John touched her hair. "Were they painkillers?"

"All drugs are, in the broadest sense."

"She moved from one to the next?"

"Right on up the scale."

Gentle fingers brushed Nina's scalp, soothing her, silently giving her strength. "Was it an overdose that finally did it?"

"Mmm-hmm. Not enough to kill, just to permanently disable." Thoughts she'd had in the hospital came back to her, thoughts about illness and death, friends, relatives. In a shaky whisper, she said, "I should see her. She's lying alone. I hated lying alone when I was sick. But she is, all the time. I should see her."

"Do you often?"

She shook her head. "Too far away. Too much work."

"Too many mixed feelings."

She met his gaze. "How did you know?"

"It follows from things you've said. You wanted her there and she wasn't. You asked her to change, and she wouldn't. You've made your life the antithesis of what hers was." He paused, his thumb tracing small circles on her temple. "Were you around when it got bad with the drugs?"

"Yes. I was in school, and working."

"Where was your father?"

Feeling the same old pain she'd lived with for years, she raised a single shoulder all the way to her ear. Slowly it slid back into place.

"Don't know?"

She shook her head.

"Do you know who he is?"

After a pause, she shook her head again.

Silently John slipped his arms beneath her and brought her up into his embrace. She went limply at first, until the need he felt took her, too. Aloneness was a painful thing. Holding and being held by another person offset that pain. Wrapping her arms around his waist, she clutched at bunches of his shirt.

At first he said nothing, and that was fine. Nina was content to listen to his heartbeat, to let it lull her and offer a comfort of its own. As though she had unburdened herself of a secret that had been weighing her down for years, she grew increasingly relaxed and mellow.

His breath was warm against her hair. "Loving a man doesn't have to be a weakness."

"It's not the loving that's bad," she breathed, "it's the depending. Men meant everything to my mother. When none of them wanted her anymore, she was broken."

"So you never want to depend on a man."

"Mmm. Right."

"You want to be self-sufficient."

"Mmm-hmm." She took in a deep breath, enjoying as much the feel of John as his scent. "I won't let myself get in that bind. Not ever."

Having said that, she felt better. She had warned John. She'd been as blunt as she could be. If he wanted to nurse her, that was fine. If he wanted to wait on her and play guardian, that was fine. She couldn't deny that the coddling was nice, given that her health wasn't yet up to snuff. But once she was well, she would be on her own again.

It was good that he understood that.

8

THE FOLLOWING MORNING, while John and J.J. were at the therapist's office, Lee came to visit. Wearing the sundress she'd worn home from the hospital—and having polished her nails, which made her feel greatly improved—Nina had progressed to sitting in the den. John didn't know that yet. She planned to surprise him with her strength when he returned at noon.

"Cute place," Lee said with a cursory sweep.

Nina thought so. She had wandered around herself, for the first time, just before Lee had arrived. There were two bedrooms in addition to the one she was in, a large kitchen, a living room, and a dining room that had been converted into the den in which they sat. Nothing was "decorated," yet everything had a lived-in look that gave a feeling of warmth. She liked that far more than she was willing to admit to Lee. So she said simply, "It's clean and functional. Nothing fancy. Definitely a man's place."

Lee nodded. She looked vaguely at the walls, then the floor, then at Nina. "So. How are you feeling?"

Nina couldn't miss the awkwardness in her friend. Unsure as to its cause, she went along with the game. "Better today. I was beginning to wonder when I'd revive. It seems like forever since I've been at work."

"It's only been a week. You still look peaked."

Nina didn't like the sound of that. Lee was usually more complimentary than not, certainly more encouraging. Something was odd. "My coloring will pick up. I may go out into the backyard later." John would never allow that, but she rather liked the idea. "So," she said, affecting her business tone of voice, "tell me what's happening at the office. Did you have any luck with the Donaldsons?"

Lee opened her briefcase. "Uh-huh. They're interested in buying."

"They are? That's great!"

Lee didn't seem terribly excited. As she busied herself looking through a pile of papers, she said, "Uh-huh. They'll be coming back with a bid later this afternoon. Four o'clock, I think it is."

"Terrific. It's been a long time that they've been looking. I'm thrilled we were finally able to please them."

"Uh-huh."

"Thanks, Lee. I really appreciate all you've done." The fact was that, at Nina's insistence, Lee would get the full commission, so it wasn't work done for free. Still Nina was grateful. By ably taking over for her, Lee was keeping her professional reputation intact. "I know how much work you've put in, not only in this case, but with all of the others this past week. You've been a good friend."

Eyes still inside her briefcase, Lee shrugged. "I have plenty of time. It's nice to be able to fill it."

That sounded odd, not like the Lee Nina knew at all. Lee wasn't one to fill every minute, the way Nina did. Though she always helped Nina out when asked, she didn't actively look for work. She had always preferred a slower pace.

Nina's mind took off in all sorts of different directions until she caught herself and asked outright, "What's wrong, Lee?"

"Nothing."

"Something is. You don't sound like you."

"I'm fine."

"You're *not*."

Retrieving her hands from the briefcase and dropping them into her lap, Lee hung her head. "You're right." Timidly she looked up, her eyes filled with tears. "Tom's moving. He's getting rid of his place here and moving to Chicago. He says it's an official transfer, but I think he's taking a whole new job. And he's not taking me. It's over, he says. It was nice, but it's over." Pulling a tissue from her sleeve, she pressed it to her nose. "You were right, Nina. You had him pegged."

Heart aching, Nina reached for her arm. "Oh, Lee..."

Sniffling around the tissue, Lee said, "You were right. You knew. And you tried to tell me, but I wouldn't listen. I thought this was it. I really did. I refused to see the truth about those long weekends away. You were that much more realistic than me."

"I just didn't want you hurt."

"You saw it coming."

"I'm jaded, but that's not always so good."

"It sure has worked for you. You're not dangling at the end of Tom Brody's line. He's a rat. All men are rats."

"Not all," Nina said. She was thinking of John, of how giving and undemanding he had been. She was lucky. Strangely so. "You'll find someone else, Lee. Someone better." She squeezed Lee's hand and continued to hold it while Lee cried for a minute longer. "Now that you're free and looking around, you'll see possibilities where there didn't seem to be any before." Unexpected things happen. Nina knew. Not that *she* was looking for a man to marry, the way Lee was. "You'll do fine."

"But I'll miss him."

"I know. But you'll keep busy. I have plenty for you to do, if you want it."

After a bit, Lee stopped sniffling. "I want it," she said with resignation.

"Good," Nina said gently. "Let's talk about Crosslyn Rise."

For the next few minutes, they did just that. Determined to take Lee's mind off Tom, Nina gave her a long list of calls to make regarding a planned launch for the next-to-last week in July. She had calls to make herself, though she didn't rush to make them the minute Lee left. Instead, indulging herself in the tiredness she felt, she turned the stereo on low to a classical station, stretched out on the sofa with her head on the soft leather cushion and took a nap.

The slam of a door woke her. She opened her eyes to see J.J. dash through the room, followed at a more sedate pace by John, who stopped the instant he saw her. "Who let you out?"

"Me." She punched up the cocoa-colored cushion under her head, but made no move to rise. From her vantage point, John was looking tall, dark and handsome. She was in no rush to change the view. "It got a little claustrophobic in the bedroom, and Lee was stopping by, so I figured I'd entertain her in style. How did everything go this morning?"

"Fine." With a slowness that came across as caution, he asked, "How did it go with Lee?"

"Really good. I gave her lots of work to do. There's not a whole lot left for me."

Seeming satisfied with that, he slipped into a chair and stretched out his legs. He was wearing shorts. Nina liked his legs. They were well formed, snugly muscled and just hairy enough.

"Did you tell her about the change in dates for the open house?" he asked.

She dragged her eyes up. "Uh-huh."

"Any problem?"

"No. She'll go along with whatever I say. My worry is more with the consortium. I feel like I'm letting them down."

"You've been sick. They would never hold that against you."

"But I've been telling them that the Rise would be on the market as of the Fourth."

"So you'll tell them differently now."

"I hate to lose those few weeks of potential selling."

"Will it really make a difference in the long run?"

"I suppose not," she conceded, then shifted her gaze to J.J. when he returned to the room. As though he'd plum run out of steam, he was walking slowly, had his thumb in his mouth and was carrying a battered teddy bear. There was something so forlorn looking about him that Nina couldn't resist holding out an arm. Without the slightest hesitation, he went to her.

Drawing him in by the waist, she said, "That's a sad-looking teddy." She fingered the bear's worn nose.

"Not sad," John informed her. "Well loved. His mother gave him that teddy not long before she died."

Nina sucked in a breath. "Does he know?"

"That it was from her? Probably not. But it's special to him. He doesn't love any of his other animals the way he does this one."

Feeling a deep ache for the little boy who would never know his mother, Nina tightened her arm around his waist. He kept up his sucking without complaint.

"What happened, John?" she asked softly. She alternately touched the bear, then the small warm fingers clutching its neck. When silence continued to come from John's direction, she raised her eyes to his. "Tell me about her."

Sitting back in the chair, he crossed an ankle over his knee. Though the pose was relaxed and his voice slow, it lacked the ease that would have normally been there. "We met in Minneapolis. I had a store there, pretty much like the one I have here. Jenna was a market analyst who had just been transferred out from New York."

He rubbed his ankle with the pad of his thumb. After a long minute, he went on. "She wasn't thrilled about the move. Even though she was high up in the office bureaucracy, she felt it was a step down. But the money was good, and she figured that if she was patient, she'd move even higher, and then, if she wanted, she could move out again, preferably back to New York. From the beginning, I knew that was what she wanted, but somehow, when we started seeing each other and then got closer, it didn't seem real."

Breaking away from Nina, J.J. crossed to the television and turned it on. With the sudden blare of sound, John jumped up, tapped the boy on the shoulder and motioned him to turn it down, which he did. John turned it even lower, then turned off the stereo, leaving little to interfere with their talk.

Nina was just noticing that the program was *Sesame Street* and that an interpreter was signing in a corner of the screen, when J.J. returned to her side. Thumb back in his mouth, arm around his teddy, he climbed onto the sofa to sit in the curve of her body.

John was quickly alert. "Is he hurting you?"

"Of course not." She ran a hand down the back of J.J.'s head, over thick, silky hair. "He's so little."

"But your stomach—"

"Is fine. He seems tired."

"He'll take a nap after lunch."

Nina nodded and looked at John expectantly. Apparently satisfied that she was comfortable, he returned to the chair. This time, his legs remained sprawled.

"I'm listening," she prompted.

Though his eyes settled on her, she was sure he was seeing another woman in her place. "I thought maybe she'd change. Even when I convinced her to have the baby, I thought she'd change. I thought for sure she'd take a look at the little kid who was her own flesh and blood, and melt."

Nina didn't know how Jenna hadn't. The little kid who was her flesh and blood was a heart stopper. "Did she have a problem right from the start?"

John nodded. "She resented him. He wasn't any bigger than a peanut and he didn't say a word, but he made her feel guilty about the time she spent working. Unfortunately, her work meant everything to her." He frowned down at his hands. "When we found out about the ears and the eyes, she couldn't take it. Just couldn't take it. It was like he had been declared a trouble-maker, so she washed her hands of everything to do with him. She started working longer hours, started taking overnight trips whenever she could. She always brought him things—little cars, balloons, teddy bears—but she figured that the less she had to see him, the better."

"What about *you*? Didn't she want to see *you*?"

The bleakness of his expression said it all. Still he added, "By that time, there wasn't much left between us."

The quiet sounds from the television filled the ensuing silence. Like a puppy snuggling in, J.J. turned sideways to lay his head on Nina's thigh. She ran a hand back and forth on his warm little shoulder, but her eyes were on John. Needing to know, she asked softly, "How did she die?"

He looked off toward the window. "She was driving home very late one night after a three-day symposium, fell asleep at the wheel and hit a tree. Death was instantaneous. No other cars were involved."

Without conscious effort, Nina drew her legs up, tucking J.J. closer to her. "Tragic," she whispered, and felt a private chill. Many a time she had returned late at night from exhausting multiday seminars. More than once, she had stopped for coffee or rolled down the window to stay awake.

John stared broodingly at the floor. "It was a waste. Our marriage wasn't any good, so we'd probably have gotten divorced, but that's the least of it. She had potential. I hated what she did—hated the way she did it with such single-mindedness—but she was good at it. A lousy mother, but good at her work."

The grudging respect was clear in his voice. In turn, Nina respected him for it. Given the way Jenna had left him and his child, he could have easily been filled with scorn.

"You must have loved her once."

He thought about that for a while. "I did, in a dreamlike kind of way. She was like a butterfly, beautiful but elusive."

"Do you miss her?"

He shook his head, and as though the bubble of the dream had burst all over again, his voice leveled. "Like I said, we'd have ended up divorced if she hadn't wrapped herself around that tree. She wasn't an easy person to live with. She was always on, always thinking work. She was always wondering who else in the office was doing what and getting where, and how it would affect her. Her mind was always working on ways she could get ahead. Work was her be-all and end-all, her raison d'être. As time went on, it only got worse."

"*I'm* not that bad," Nina said with feeling, then caught herself, realizing what she'd done. Defensively she said, "You compare us. I know you do."

His eyes held hers steadily. "Do you wonder why?"

In an attempt to be fair, she shrugged. "I can see some similarities. She worked a lot, I work a lot. She was trying to get ahead, so am I. But I'd never have done what she did. I'd never have turned my back on a child. Or a husband. There are responsibilities involved when you marry and have kids. You shouldn't do either, if you want to work."

"It's all or nothing, then?" John shot back with startling speed. "Either you marry and have kids, or you work? No middle ground?"

"Sometimes no, sometimes yes. It depends on where you are in life. I'm at the work stage. I'm not saying that I'll never get married and have kids, just that I wouldn't take on either of those now."

"You couldn't compromise? You couldn't make time for all of it?"

"There are only so many hours in a day, and you're the one who's been telling me I work too much. Where would I find the time to give to a husband or kids?"

He remained quiet.

"Where?" she demanded. If he was putting her on the spot, she could do the same to him.

"You make time for what you want," he stated in a voice that was deafeningly clear. "You give a little here, give a little there. It may mean that one thing or another takes longer to achieve, but it all comes out in the wash."

"'One thing or another,'" Nina echoed. "You mean work. If a woman is willing to sacrifice her career, she can have the husband and kids."

"She doesn't have to sacrifice the career," he insisted, "just defer the ultimate gratification. And that doesn't mean there isn't gratification along the way, simply that the achievements may not be as high until the kids are grown and out of the house."

"She's an old lady by then."

"No way." He sat back and linked his fingers, seeming more relaxed, as though confident he had the argument won. "Take that woman. She had kids in her mid-twenties. They're out on their own by the time she's fifty. Fifty is not old."

"It's too old to start building a career."

"She's not starting. She started years ago. She may have taken a leave when the kids were babies, but after that she worked part-time, maybe full-time as the kids got older. Okay, so she didn't go running off on business trips, or push past a forty-hour week, and maybe that held her back a little. But look what she *has*. She has a solid career. She has a solid marriage. She has kids who probably give her more satisfaction than anything she does at work. And she's only fifty."

With barely a breath, he raised a hand and went on. "Then again, take the woman who put her career before everything else. She got out of school, entered the marketplace and worked her tail off. She started climbing the ladder of success, and the drive became self-perpetuating. The higher she climbed, the higher she wanted to be. The more money she earned, the more she needed. There was always something more, always something more."

"Her being a woman didn't help," Nina put in. "A woman has to work twice as hard."

To her surprise, John agreed. "You're right. And that made her all the *more* determined to make it. So she put off thoughts of getting married, since she didn't have time for that. And she put off having kids, because she didn't have time for *that*. Then she reaches her mid-forties, when theoretically she should be up there on the threshold of the president's office, only there are suddenly four other candidates vying for the job and one of them is the new son-in-law of the chairman of the board. So she misses out. And then what does she have?" He raised a finger. "She doesn't have the corner office." Then another. "She doesn't have a husband." Then a third. "And her childbearing years are gone." He dropped his hand to his lap. "Do you think she's happy?"

His eloquence left Nina momentarily speechless.

"She's alone, Nina," he said more quietly. "She's alone, and she's getting older, and she's beginning to wonder what she'll do with herself if she ever has to retire. Happy? My guess is she's scared to death."

Tearing her eyes from his, Nina looked down at the floor. Aloneness was something that had flashed through her mind more than once when she'd been in the hospital. Different people had dropped by to visit, but John had been a constant in her life. Without him, she would have felt very much alone.

She wondered what, if anything, her mother felt sitting in that nursing home day after day. The doctors had said that she didn't know who or where she was, or who came and went, but Nina had always had a niggling fear in the back of her mind that maybe it wasn't so. Over the years, she had successfully kept the fear hidden in a dark corner of her mind. She was a lousy daughter.

Feeling suddenly very much an imposter in a haven she didn't deserve, she looked at John. "Why am I here?"

He frowned. "What do you mean?"

"From the beginning, I reminded you of Jenna. I'm everything you had once and couldn't stand. I'm a repeat of a mistake. So what am I doing here, interfering with your life?"

"You're here because I want you here."

"But why?"

"Because I like you."

"But I'll only cause you grief."

"Maybe not."

"What does *that* mean?" she cried.

John didn't answer for a while, but sat quietly, eyes downcast, brows drawn together, and Nina didn't prod. She was feeling tired again. Turning her head into the cushion, she closed her eyes.

His voice came gently. "I like you, Nina. Yes, you're right, you did remind me of Jenna, but only at the start and only with regard to work. In other ways, you're different. She was tall, blond and green eyed, you're blue eyed, dark and petite. She dressed to fit in, you dress to stand out. She smiled on cue, you smile whenever you want to. You're your own person far more than she ever was."

Nina had opened those blue eyes and was looking at him, feeling a longing that was only in part physical. "But I love my work."

He nodded. "Yes, you do."

"And you hate that."

Again he nodded.

"So why are you *bothering* with me?"

"Because," he said with a somber look and a surprising lack of hesitancy, "I like you enough to care. I'm not sure I felt that way about Jenna. I may have loved her once, but I didn't like her. When she was barging headlong toward self-destruction, I did nothing to stop her."

"You were busy with J.J."

"True, but I could have tried more if I'd cared. Then again, Jenna was a hard woman. She wouldn't have listened. Once she set her mind to something, she wouldn't budge." His eyes softened a fraction. "You're not as hard. As determined as you are, you still listen."

She gave a small self-conscious laugh. "I haven't exactly had much choice lately."

"Even before you got sick, you listened. You didn't want to work with me, but you agreed to do it. You made time for it even though you said you couldn't. Besides that, you're more sensitive than Jenna ever was. You feel badly when I have to get a sitter for J.J. in order to see you. You worry that you're going to do something wrong when it comes to him. Look at you," he said with the hitch of his chin, "you've been touching him in some small way, just like a seasoned mother, ever since we got back, and I don't think you even realize it."

Startled, Nina shot a glance at J.J., who was curled up in the curve of her body. Her hand was on his arm, the backs of her fingers brushing ever so lightly over the baby-smooth skin.

When she returned her gaze to John, he was looking satisfied. Pushing out of his chair, he bent over her, putting his mouth by her ear. "Not bad, for someone who doesn't know what to do with kids." On his way to straightening, he scooped J.J. up. "Lunchtime, my man," he said.

J.J., who had neither heard him nor seen his lips, made a loud sound in protest and started to squirm. John immediately set him on his feet and hunkered down before him. "Time for lunch," he mouthed clearly. He tapped his wrist with a finger, then mimed bringing food to his mouth.

J.J. looked questioningly back at Nina.

"She'll come, too," John assured him with a nod, gave him a pat on the bottom and stood. To Nina, he said, "Want to?"

"Sure. What are we having?"

John caught J.J.'s eye. "What do you want to eat?" he asked slowly, signing along with the words.

J.J. made the sign for spaghetti.

John shook his head. "We had that for supper last night."

J.J. made a stirring motion with one hand, then tapped the back of his fist with two fingers.

Again John shook his head. "Mashed potatoes alone aren't enough."

J.J. drew large twin arches in the air.

John chuckled. "Not McDonald's. How about a surprise?" He formed two fingers of both hands into curved Vs, put the fingertips together, then drew them apart with a look of surprise.

J.J. said something that wasn't any kind of word Nina had ever heard but sounded agreeable nonetheless, particularly when he clapped.

"Okay," John finger-spelled, then repeated the gesture for Nina. "I would have spelled out 'bologna,' except that it's too hard a word for him to read. Is bologna okay for you?"

"It's my favorite," she said with a smile, feeling warm and amenable and all kinds of other nice things. The rapport between John and his son was delightful. Being part of their group, undeserved though it was and brief though it would be, was an honor.

AFTER LUNCH SHE NAPPED, then John surprised her by suggesting that, while J.J. was with his sitters and he was at work, she sit out in the backyard. "Great minds think alike," she said. "I told Lee I wanted to sit there, but I didn't think you'd let me."

"You look too pale. You need some color." The corner of his mouth turned wry. "We wouldn't want people to think you've been sick, now, would we?"

"Certainly not," Nina said, but no sooner was she settled in a chaise lounge, in the dappled sun that danced through the oak boughs, when she thought of what he'd said. He'd been facetious, of course. But, in fact, the rest of the world was waiting. She did have to get back to work.

She'd have to discuss that with John, she knew, but she wasn't looking forward to it. He would tell her she wasn't well yet, and she would feel obligated to say she was getting there fast, and it would go back and forth, as arguments went. In the end, he would wear her down, simply because she wasn't feeling up to par. So, valid or not, he'd have made his point.

Telling herself that she had time to spare, she didn't say a word for the rest of that day. Rather, she lay in and out of the sun for several hours, dozing at some points, watching J.J. play at others. For a time, curious to see what he was doing and how, she sat on the edge of his sandbox and helped him make sand castles. She had as much fun with the sand as she did with J.J. and didn't feel either bothered or frightened to be left alone with him when his sitters went back inside for cold drinks. He was a gentle little boy with the calm temperament of his father. With simple hand motions and facial expressions, she found she could communicate with him just fine.

For dinner, John grilled swordfish steaks, and though J.J. wasn't wild about his, Nina ate every bite. J.J. was wild about dessert, though, a chocolate cake that John had bought at the bakery that morning, and while Nina was watching him eat, John got up to do the dishes. When she offered to help, he refused.

"I didn't insist that you come here, just to put you to work."

"I'm not helpless," she protested.

"But you've been sick."

She wanted to point out that anyone who was well enough to sunbathe and build sand castles could probably handle a few pots and pans, but she didn't. Anyone who could handle a few pots and pans could probably do the cooking as well, which meant that she really should be heading home. But she wasn't ready for that just yet. John kept telling her that she was weak, that she needed more rest, that she had to take it slow if she wanted to regain all her strength. She chose to believe him.

THE BELIEVING WAS all well and good on Saturday. John was in the bookstore all day. J.J. was in and out with sitters. Nina slept a bit, read a bit, boiled up chicken breasts and made chicken salad sandwiches for lunch as a surprise for John.

He was furious. "I don't want you working."

"But I'm feeling stronger, and I'm bored. Honestly, John, what I did was no effort. I'm standing better and walking better. Besides, I have all afternoon to rest."

The look he gave her said that she'd better do just that, but she noticed with satisfaction that he ate every last bite of his sandwich before he returned to the store. Buoyed by that, she did rest awhile. When she woke up, she finished the book he had given to her to read, then went back into the kitchen and cooked up a batch of chocolate chip cookies.

J.J. Sawyer might have had vision and hearing problems, but nothing was wrong with his sense of smell. The cookies were still in the oven when he followed his nose there. He was positively ebullient when she let him peek through the glass.

John's sense of smell was nearly as keen. At the first lull in business, he too materialized in the kitchen, where, hands on his hips, he surveyed the scene. Two fifteen-year-old girls, J.J. and Nina were sitting at the table having an orgy of cookies and milk.

"Better hurry," Nina warned. "They won't last long."

"Should I ask who made them?"

"No."

Eagerly standing up on his chair, J.J. held out a half-eaten cookie to his father. "Are they good?" John asked in sign.

Nodding vigorously, J.J. continued to hold out the cookie until John reached for it, and, with a mischievous grin, he promptly stuffed it in his mouth.

"You devil," his father said, and reached for a cookie of his own. He made a show of taking a bite and thinking about the taste, before downing the rest of the cookie in one large bite.

"You're as bad as he is," Nina said as she rose from the table. Taking J.J.'s eyeglasses from his nose, she washed a chocolate streak from one lens, rinsed and dried both, then carefully slipped them back on. She bent over to study her handiwork. "Better?" Her eyes shot to John's. "How do I sign that?"

He showed her. She repeated the two-part gesture to J.J., who returned it. Eminently pleased with herself and the situation, she took up a napkin, filled it with cookies and handed it to John. "For work," she said.

In a typically John way, he looked at the cookies, looked at her, then slowly took the small bundle. "Thanks," was all he said before he returned to the store.

NINA THOUGHT A LOT about that "thanks" during the rest of the day. Even more, she thought about the look that had gone with it, because it hadn't held gratitude so much as puzzlement, even frustration, if she guessed right. But what could she tell him? She liked to bake so she'd baked cookies, which was no more than she might have done if she had been home and snowed in on a winter weekend with no hope of getting to work.

Maybe he was thinking that she wanted to impress him.

Maybe he was thinking that she wanted to impress J.J.

Maybe he was thinking that she was well enough to leave.

She was. She really was. Come Saturday night, when she stayed awake through the entire movie he rented, she knew it. Come Sunday morning, when she put on the bathing suit he'd picked up at her apartment and spent the day—albeit restfully—at the beach with J.J. and him, she knew it. Come Sunday evening, lolling around on the sofa, trying to read but thinking instead about the irresistible lure of John's body, she knew it.

John knew it, too, because shortly after she said good-night and stole off to her room, he appeared at her door. Little more than a shadow in the night, he crossed to the bed and sat down. No longer a shadow then, he took her in his arms.

Senses that had been gradually reviving over the course of the past few days came fully awake. With a soft moan, Nina slid her arms around his neck. He was so wonderful to hold, so solid, so gentle, virile in everything from his shape to his scent. She felt so alive, restored, whole in mystifying ways.

"I missed this," he murmured. "All the time you've been here, I've wanted to hold you. It was toughest at the beach today. You looked so pretty."

She swallowed against a swell of emotion.

"You want to leave."

"I don't, but I can't stay. I'm getting better. Every day."

For the first time, he didn't refute her argument. Instead, he said, "It's a rat race out there. You don't belong in it."

"I do. It's where I've always been."

"Only because you had no other choice. But you do now. I want you to stay here, Nina. I want you to stay here with me."

Her heart contracted. "Oh, John."

"What does that mean?"

"I *can't*. I can't just give up everything I've spent a lifetime working for."

Pulling back, he took her face in his hands. "I'm not asking you to give everything up, just to add some things. You've been happy here. I know you have. You made up your mind that you couldn't work, and you were happy here."

"But now I *can* work. Maybe not full-time yet, but certainly half-time."

"So go to work from here."

"I can't."

"Why not?"

Unable to resist, she touched his mouth. "Because I'd feel guilty. I've always been independent. I come and go as I please. I can't be doing that from your home. Especially now."

"What does that mean?"

Her fingers moved aside. Inching up, she touched her lips to his, simply because she needed to feel him that way. When she drew back, she knew that what she was about to say was the frightening truth. "Now I'd be tempted, so tempted to play with you. I'd be tempted to lie around reading all night, or spend the afternoon making sand castles, or bake us all into obesity. It's been nice here, so nice, but I have to leave. If I don't, I won't get where I want to be, and if I don't get where I want to be, I might come to resent you, and I'd never want to do that, John."

Amber eyes alive in the dark, he moved his gaze around her face. He followed the eye motion with that of a hand. His voice was low and sandy. "It isn't right that it should be one or the other. You'll be hurt, Nina. I don't want that."

"No hurt," she said, but the accompanying shake of her head was cut short when his hand slipped lower to her neck, then lower still to the budding swell of her breast. She bit down on her lip to stifle a moan.

"You like that?" he whispered. His large hand circled her, moving inward in slow, concentric rings.

"Oh, yes," she whispered back. "You have a way with my body."

"At least I have that."

"You have more—" she began, but the words died when he touched one taut nipple. Another moan came from her throat, this one slipping free into the air.

"Do I hurt you?"

"Only by making me want more."

"Your stomach—"

"No, no." Covering his hand, she pressed it close. "You set me on fire."

The night hid his expression, but the catch of his breath told of what she'd missed. Gently he lowered her to the bed. His mouth followed, capturing hers in a kiss that opened gently, as did her body. Taking advantage of that opening, his hands loved her breasts through the silk of her thin nightie. She felt herself swell to his touch, felt the ache of wanting in her nipples, then lower. Arching upward, she tried to bring him down, but he held himself steadily over her while his hands continued their sweet torture.

The doctor had told her, before leaving the hospital, that her body would tell her when sex was okay. At the time, she'd felt numb and sore. Passion had seemed a distant phenomenon, not the least bit appealing to her bruised and mending self.

Five days of rest and tender care at John's hand had made a world of difference. Though she could feel the intermittent tugging in stomach muscles that contracted with desire, the sensation blended in with her need.

"I want you," she whispered, and slid her hands down his thighs. She was making the upward journey to his groin when he caught her hands and pinned them by her shoulders.

Holding both wrists, he seduced her mouth with a series of deep soul kisses. Then he worked his way down and applied that devastatingly capable mouth to her breasts. From one hard tip to the other he moved, using his tongue, his teeth, his fingers. The wetter her nightie grew, the hotter she grew inside.

When he slipped his hand under the shirt and touched her between her legs, she cried out.

"Hurting?" he asked in concern.

"With need." She grabbed his wrist to stop him. "Make love to me, John." She arched toward his hips but was only able to make the briefest, glancing contact with his erection when he pinned her down.

"It's too soon."

"No. No. I want you inside."

"Too soon," he repeated, and levered himself up enough to return his hand to her cleft. "This way," he whispered, taking her mouth in an enveloping kiss at the same time that his fingers found their way to her darkest heat.

She was lost then. The best she could do was to flex frantic fingers on his back while he built the fire inside her to an explosive level. He stroked her inside and out, up and down, back and forth, until her shallow breathing caught and she was shot to the pinnacle of orgasmic release.

Her return to reality was a slow one. By the time she could finally open her eyes, she was being cradled against John's supine body. The pervasive weakness she felt told her that, much as she wanted to make love to him back, she wouldn't be doing it that night.

Her "Oh, John" was a soulful sound.

Silently he stroked her hair.

Gradually the trembling of her body eased, leaving a great fatigue in its place. "I want ... I want ..." The words were slurred, the thoughts behind them muddled.

It wasn't until dawn Monday, when she woke up wanting John and finding herself alone in bed, that those thoughts jelled.

9

BY THE TIME she heard waking sounds in the rest of the house, Nina had dressed, gathered her belongings and packed her small bag. As soon as those other sounds moved into the kitchen, she headed there, too.

John was at the stove frying eggs. At the sight of him, she felt an ache start inside. It had nothing to do with her recent surgery and everything to do with her growing feeling for the man she had to leave.

She hadn't been standing at the door for more than a few seconds when he looked her way, not the least bit startled. She guessed that he'd been expecting her.

Returning his attention to the eggs, he scooped one onto a plate, added a piece of toast and set the breakfast in front of J.J., who was on his knees on a chair at the table.

Looking at the little boy, Nina felt another ache. She had growing feeling for him, too, and that was even more surprising than the other. She had liked John for a while now; in the past ten days, her feelings had only intensified. J.J., on the other hand, had been a stranger up until the Thursday before. Stranger? *Alien being* was more apt. He was a child and he had problems. She had never lived with a child before, let alone one with problems. It hadn't been anywhere near as bad as she'd thought it would be.

Sliding into a chair beside the little one, she stroked his head in wordless "good morning." When he grinned up at her, she grinned back. When he picked up a piece of his toast and offered it, she shook her head and the ache inside grew.

"You're leaving," John said quietly.

She nodded. "I have to."

He could have argued, she knew, but he didn't. They had been through the arguments and exhausted each one. Nothing had changed.

"Will you have breakfast first?"

Though she wasn't terribly hungry, she wasn't denying herself a few last moments of the particular pleasure of being with J.J. and John. "Only if you have enough."

"There are two more eggs here. We'll each have one. Same with the toast."

Clearly he hadn't made extra, hadn't expected that she'd eat. "Oh, no," she said quickly, "you have them. I didn't mean to take—"

He interrupted her with a level stare and a firm, "We'll share. I don't mind. One egg is more than enough for me, and even if it weren't, I don't mind giving a little."

The emphasis on the last few words and the message therein was mirrored in his look. He was saying that life didn't have to be all or nothing, that he was more than willing to compromise if she was.

But she wasn't. Though she nodded yes to the egg and accepted the plate he offered without a word, she felt guilty. She couldn't compromise. She *couldn't*. For too long, she had wanted her independence. With Crosslyn Rise about to go on the market, she was coming close to her goal, too close to give it up.

But what she was giving up on the other end—that was where it was starting to hurt. Her feelings for John were strong and growing more so with each day. To stay would be asking for trouble. Already she wanted things she couldn't have.

I want to make love to you. I want to spend the night with you. I want to stay here forever. Those were the words she might have said if she hadn't been so spent from his loving the night before. Then again, if she'd been in full control of her senses, she wouldn't have said them at all. Leading John on, giving him cause to hope for something that couldn't be, would be cruel.

Did she mean the words? Yes. That was what she'd realized at dawn, why she knew she had to leave. She did want all those things. But she wanted her self-sufficiency more. In her mind—right or wrong—to be dependent on John would be a sign of weakness. She prided herself on being stronger than that.

"Are you going right back to work?" he asked quietly.

She pushed at the deckled edge of her egg. "Tomorrow, I think. I'll get home today, maybe make a few calls. As soon as I get tired, I'll stop." Unspoken was the fact that as long as she felt all right, she'd keep at it. John knew she would. He had experience with her type.

He bit hard into his toast, chewed, swallowed, took another bite.

"We have a consortium meeting next week," she said in an open-ended kind of way. When he didn't respond, she said, "Will I see you before then?"

He shrugged. "Do you want to?"

She was asking herself the same question. On one hand, the thought of not seeing him at all was bleak. One the other hand, perhaps a clean break was for the best.

But they were friends, weren't they? And they'd just come through a harrowing experience together. Surely he'd want to know that she was all right. "I think I'd like to talk. You know, see how things are going here and all."

"Then why don't you call when you have time." With barely a break, he said, "Eat your egg. It's getting cold."

At first she thought he was talking to J.J., but J.J.'s egg was gone. Seconds later, J.J. was gone, too, off to play in his room.

Nina ate her egg. Not at all hungry for the toast, she held it out as a peace offering to John, but he shook his head, so she put the plate down. He was angry. Maybe hurt. Maybe disdainful again. He wanted her to stay, and she wouldn't. She wouldn't meet him halfway. He had a right to be upset, she supposed, after all he'd done for her.

But that was exactly the kind of thinking that could get a woman into trouble, she knew. So, rather than apologize or try to explain things she'd already tried to explain more than once, she said, "I'd better call a cab, I guess."

John's reaction was fast and furious. "You don't need any damn cab. I'll drive you home." With the scrape of his chair, he rose from the table and carried the plates to the sink.

She met him there. "Let me do that. You can take care of J.J."

"J.J.'s all ready to go," he said, and began loading the dishwasher.

"Then do something else. Let me *help* for a change."

He rounded on her with such suddenness that she took a startled step back. "I don't need your help. I don't need *anyone's* help. You're not the only one who likes to be independent and self-sufficient."

Feeling duly chastised, she said a quiet, "I know. I was just trying to help. You've done so much—"

"And I never asked for a thing in return. I never *expected* a thing in return. So don't feel you owe me, because you don't. I did what I wanted to do, what *I* wanted to do."

When he turned back to the sink with a vengeance, Nina silently withdrew from the room. She got her bag, dropped it by the door, then, without conscious intent, found herself looking in on J.J. He was standing in front of a low bookshelf, on the top of which was a large drawing pad. With crayons from a nearby box, he was making random marks on the pad.

Approaching, she saw that the marks weren't random at all, but his version of letters. There was a wide assortment of them in various shades and sizes, but her eyes were drawn to two deep blue ones, bolder and more distinct than the others, two *J*s.

Grinning, Nina pointed to them. "Look at that. Good boy, J.J." Remembering what John had done, she signed the word "good," then clapped her hands together. Then, while J.J. was beaming with pride, she took a bright pink crayon and wrote her own name. "*N-I-N-A.* Nina." She pointed from the name to herself and back several times, then gently tipped up J.J.'s chin to see if he understood. "Nina," she mouthed, pointing again to herself.

He repeated the mouth exactly.

"Good boy!" she signed, then arched her brows and pointed questioningly at herself.

He mouthed her name a second time, this time pointing to her as he did it.

Grinning widely, she grabbed his hand, brought it to her mouth and gave it a smacking kiss. Then she hauled him in and gave him a full-fledged hug while he giggled and squirmed. She'd miss him, she knew.

But she'd miss his father even more.

HER APARTMENT WAS QUIET, the same yet strange. She wandered from room to room, trailing her fingertips over the furniture, trying to reacquaint herself with possessions that were familiar, until she realized that she was the one that was strange. She had been away for a week and a half. A week and a half. Not much. Then again, a long time.

John had insisted on stopping at the market on the way for fresh food so that she wouldn't have to go out, but the emptiness she felt wasn't from hunger. She climbed into bed, thinking that maybe after a nap she'd feel more like herself. When an hour passed and she couldn't sleep, she got up, opened her appointment book and picked up the phone.

Work was what she needed, she knew. It had always been her greatest source of satisfaction. It was what made her tick.

Sure enough, after calling first the office, then several clients to tell them she was back on track, she was feeling fuller. Liking that feeling, she made more calls and would have made even more if she hadn't been legitimately tired by then.

This time she slept, and when she woke up, she made more calls. When she ran out of calls to make, she dialed John's number, only to hang up before the phone had rung. Calling him so soon after she'd seen him was a weak thing to do. She was fine on her own, just fine.

As though to prove that to herself, she grabbed pen and paper and began to organize her thoughts for the rest of the week. With each note she took and each list she made, she felt more convinced that what she was doing was right. Work was *definitely* what she needed. It was the best medicine money could buy.

THE FOLLOWING MORNING, telling herself how great it was to be out and moving around on her own once again, she drove to the office. She didn't stay long, only long enough to let everyone know she was back and ready to work. Armed with a computer printout of the latest listings, she spent the rest of the morning viewing the new entries. By then, to her chagrin, she felt drained. So she went back home, changed out of her dress into shorts and spent the afternoon lounging on the living room sofa, feeling blue.

That was why she didn't call John. She refused to go running to him when she was down. She could pick herself up. She always had before, and she would again.

WEDNESDAY MORNING, things were better. Feeling just that little bit stronger, she took several clients out for showings. By noon, though, she'd had it. She slept most of the afternoon away, picked at the dinner she had halfheartedly cooked, then spent the evening trying to get into one of the books she had brought home from John's. But she was distracted. She kept thinking of him, wondering what he was doing and whether he was thinking of her—then chastising herself for the thoughts. She'd made her choice. She would just have to live with it.

And damn it, if he wanted to talk with her, *he* could call.

THURSDAY MORNING, after showing two clients five separate pieces of real estate with little more than a nibble of interest, she went out to Crosslyn Rise. She needed uplifting. Crosslyn Rise could give her that.

The mansion was moving along nicely. It occurred to her that with the open house pushed back those two extra weeks, something impressive might well be done here. Her mind shifted into gear, turning the possibilities around and around. Pulling a notepad from her bag, she jotted down some ideas.

Then she headed for the duck pond, where the first cluster of eight condominiums was nearing completion, and she was struck, truly struck, by the beauty of the place. The outside hadn't changed drastically since she'd seen it last. She still loved the modified Georgian design, the hints of pillars and balconies, the sloped roofs that hid rear skylights, the cedar shingles painted taupe with cream trim. But something was different. Lowering herself to the ground with her back braced against a tree, she pondered that difference.

After a long time, during which she stretched her legs out in the sun, followed the antics of an occasional duck and breathed deeply of air redolent with the smell of grass, new wood and nature, she realized that it was the trees. With the start of summer, they were fuller and richer than they had been. And the lawn. Sod that had been put down where men and machines had mangled the earth had taken root and was now a deep, healthy green. And the shrubbery. Christine had worked with a landscaper on that, and between them, they had created a masterpiece of color and texture. As the icing on the cake, the greenery worked.

For the first time, Nina wished she could afford one of the units herself. There was something so peaceful about the place. Everything that had been done was of high quality and refined—everything Nina might have let herself dream of owning, but hadn't. She'd always had other dreams. They came first.

Sitting there in the sun, though, lulled by the smells of the outdoors and the sounds of the ducks and the nearby ocean, she didn't want to think about those other dreams. She just wanted to *be*.

Which, to her surprise, was exactly what she proceeded to do for what had to have been nearly half an hour, before two people emerged from the model condominium and approached her.

Tipping her head back against the bark of the old maple, she grinned. "Hey, you guys, what's been goin' on in there?"

Christine shot her husband a mischievous look. "Nothing much—"

"—through no fault of mine," Gideon cut in. "But Chris is all business when it comes to this place. She wants everything done, and done right, in time for your show."

"How are you feeling, Nina?"

Other than squinting against the sun, Nina didn't move. "Fine. Lazy. This place is like a drug. I'm in awe that you both manage to get work done here. Every time I come, I get sidetracked."

This time, the mischievous look Chris sent Gideon was reflected right back. "We know the feeling," she said, then took a deep breath and tore her eyes from his to look at Nina again. "You're looking good. It's hard to believe you went through what you did only two weeks ago."

"I had good care. I was lucky."

"John was pretty worried about you," Gideon said, more serious now. "When he called to tell us you were sick, he was upset."

Nina chuckled. "He was laying it on thick, so none of you would dare ask me when I'd be getting back to work."

"He was right about the open house, though," Chris put in. "It can just as easily wait until the end of the month."

Gideon draped an arm around his wife's shoulder. To Nina, in a conspiratorial voice, he said, "Especially since the fabric of the living room furniture in the model came through wrong. Chris has been sweating bullets about that. With the few extra weeks, it'll be fixed."

"So. Are you guys buying one of the units?"

They exchanged a meaningful look. It was Gideon who said, "We've been sorely tempted. It'd be a gorgeous place to live in. But Chris's daughter is still in high school. It wouldn't be fair to uproot her and tear her away from her friends—"

"And then there's this little matter of Gideon's dream," Chris put in, looking up at him again. "He's been waking up in the middle of the night with the notion that once Jill graduates we should sell his place in Worcester, buy land somewhere and build a spectacular house of our own."

"It's not a notion," Gideon argued. "It's a full-fledged plan. I can picture the whole house. Hell, I've got the basics already down on paper. It may take us a while to get it built, but when it's done, it'll be super."

He kissed Chris lightly on the lips and looked as though he wanted to do more, when Chris offered a soft, "If we don't get going, we'll be late." To Nina she said, "We're meeting Carter and Jessica for a late lunch. You know that Jessica's pregnant, don't you?"

Nina nodded. "I'm thrilled for her."

"So are we." As they started off, she added, "Listen, I'll give you a call in a day or two. Don't work too hard, Nina. We want you well."

Nina raised a hand in a wave, then let if fall to her lap as Chris and Gideon went farther up the path toward the mansion. She was thrilled for them, too. They were clearly so pleased to be together, so very much in love.

Sitting there, she felt a smidgeon of envy. Christine Lowe had it all—a husband, a daughter, a career. Jessica Malloy was on her way, too. Gideon and Carter were both fine men.

So was John. Fine, and kind, and smart, and sexy.

Feeling, at the very moment, an intense urge to touch him, she moaned aloud. She hadn't seen him since Monday morning. She missed him. Indeed, she'd been missing him all week. It occurred to her that the idea of making a clean break had sounded good but it wasn't much fun.

She deserved a little fun once in a while, didn't she? A little fun wouldn't be compromising her independence, would it?

Determined to call him that night, she pushed up against the tree trunk, returned to her car and drove home. By the time she got there, she knew that a call wouldn't be enough. She wanted to see John. Just a short visit. A drop-in visit. Just to see how he was getting on. And how J.J. was getting on. She could say hello, then leave with her sense of independence and self-sufficiency intact.

SHE WENT SHORTLY AFTER SEVEN. The Leaf Turner was closed then, dinner would be over, and though there was a chance that John might have taken J.J. out for ice cream, she figured that with his bedtime approaching, they'd be back soon.

Her heart did a soft flip-flop when she saw the car parked back by the garage. Driving up to the side door, she rang the bell, then stuck her head inside. "John?" she called. Hearing no response, she went up the stairs.

She found them in the bathroom. John was giving J.J. a bath, though it was questionable who was the wetter of the two. For a minute she just stood at the door and watched. They were an adorable pair, playing under the guise of rinsing. Aside from the sounds that weren't quite like those of other children, J.J. looked like a happy, normal child. But it was to John that her eye kept returning. He looked wonderful, pleasantly wet and mussed, capable, strong. Thanks to the water, his shirt and shorts were clinging to his body more lovingly than they might otherwise have done. To her hungry eyes, he looked extraordinarily masculine.

Suffused with a warm glow inside, she asked, "What's going on here?"

John's head flew around at the sound of her voice. His sudden movement alerted J.J. to her presence. Though the child wasn't wearing his glasses, he must have recognized her overall color and shape, because with the splash of water and a nasal squeal, he began to jump up and down.

"Easy," John said, turning quickly back to him and grabbing an arm. "You'll slip if you're not careful." He said it more to himself, because with one hand on J.J. and another groping for a towel, he couldn't sign. Not that that would have worked, anyway. J.J.'s eyes were riveted to Nina.

Nina was the one who grabbed the towel and shook it open. "Lift him out," she said, "and I'll wrap him up."

John did that, and within seconds, J.J. was enveloped in a warm terry-cloth cocoon. Nina gave him a hug, only to pull quickly back when he complained in the most vociferous of ways. "Oops, what'd I do?"

"You wrapped up his arms," John explained quietly. "He can't communicate without them."

J.J. had already set about remedying the situation by pushing his way out of the towel. Then his little arms reached for her and his little body followed close by. Even if Nina had been wearing her fanciest dress rather than shorts and a T-shirt, she wouldn't have minded the dampness or warmth. Grabbing J.J. around the bare back and bottom, rocking him from side to side, she felt she was holding something more valuable than any property title that had ever passed through her hands. He was precious. He was alive. He was a special, special little boy.

Her eyes rose to John, who was standing near where she knelt. He was regarding her somberly, seeming unsure as to what to make of her arrival.

"I just wanted to stop by and say hi," she explained softly. "To see how you are."

"We're fine," he said as somberly as he was looking. "We weren't the ones who were sick."

"Well, I'm fine, too," she said, but no sooner were the words out than J.J. pulled back and began making sounds. His small hand was at work finger-spelling something, but far too quickly for her to follow, even if she had known the manual alphabet, which she didn't. Something about the sounds, though, the repetition of the syllables, began to ring a bell. Not knowing whether to believe what she was hearing, she looked wide-eyed up at John, who explained.

"He wrote your name for the therapist. She had him practice finger-spelling it, but he wanted to say it, too." Begrudgingly, Nina thought, he added, "It isn't often that he voluntarily speaks. You should feel honored."

"I do," Nina breathed. Looking back at J.J., she grinned and nodded vigorously, then gave him another hard hug, followed by a kiss, followed by, "*Very* honored."

John didn't sound terribly impressed. "It's nice you stopped by so he could try it out on you. He's been asking all week where you were."

She raised stricken eyes to John's, but he turned on his heel, muttering something about getting pajamas, and left the bathroom. Holding J.J. back, Nina put a finger to the tip of his nose, mouthed, "Thank you," then, tucking him into the curve of her arm, pulled the plug on the water in the tub. When he reached over to take out his rubber duckie, she saw an ugly scrape on his elbow. Forming her mouth into a dismayed "Oh," she took the arm in her hand. "Boo-boo?"

J.J. nodded and signed something that she couldn't understand. She was telling herself that she'd have to learn more signs, when John returned.

"He did that yesterday. Came fast off the slide and scraped it. It hurt."

Gently Nina lifted the scraped elbow and put a feather-light kiss to it. "I'm sorry."

Retrieving the towel, John began to dry J.J.'s back. "It's part of growing up."

"It must hurt you, too, when it happens." She could feel the sting herself.

"Uh-huh."

Little by little, J.J.'s small body disappeared into his pajamas. Sitting back on her heels, Nina watched. She half wished she had someone to take care of like John had J.J. She didn't have the time, of course; still there had been something nice about that warm little body snuggling close.

With a flurry of hands, John and J.J. began to talk to each other. Nina waited patiently, wishing she knew more about signing, making up her mind to learn. Finally John looked at her.

"How long were you planning to stay?" he asked in a neutral tone of voice.

Wanting to stay awhile, but, thanks to that neutral tone, unsure of her welcome, she shrugged. "Did you have plans?"

"J.J. wants you in on a good-night story. He wants you to hold the book and turn the pages, while I sign."

"I'd love to," she said with pleasure. John might not have been thrilled to see her, but if J.J. was, that was a start. She'd steal time with John any way she could.

The next fifteen minutes were near to heaven. Sitting on J.J.'s bed with the small child nestled close to her side, Nina watched John sign the story of *The Little Engine That Could* as she read it aloud. She knew the story. Her first-grade teacher had loved it, and she had loved her first-grade teacher, so she'd always remembered the book.

She wondered whether John had chosen it for a reason. With its theme of the small engine that, against all odds and by dint of sheer determination, made its way over the mountain to deliver toys and games to the little boys and girls on the other side, it suggested to J.J. that he could do whatever he wanted if he was determined enough.

It suggested the same thing to Nina.

She was still thinking about that when the book was over. A sleepy J.J. gave her a big hug and a kiss, then turned to his father. Not wanting to intrude on their private good-night, Nina quietly left the room. She was leaning against the wall in the hall, with her arms wrapped around her middle, when he joined her.

His look was quelling. "He wanted to know if he could go in and see you in the morning. I had to explain that you wouldn't be here." Without giving her a chance to reply, he took off down the stairs.

Silently she followed. He had a right to be upset on J.J.'s behalf, she knew. But she would have liked it if *he* had been pleased to see her.

He hadn't said a word to that effect. Nor had anything in his look said that he was glad she had come—except maybe for his surprise when he'd first seen her, maybe there had been a little pleasure in that.

He went straight on into the bookstore, to the cartons stacked there, waiting to be unpacked. "It's hard for a kid to understand why someone he likes is there one day and gone the next."

"I know."

His gaze was cutting. "You should, if what you told me about your mother was true."

"It is. But I didn't think J.J. would make such a close tie in such a short time."

"Neither did I, or believe me, I'd never have let you stay here. But it worked between you and him. You're so totally without preconceptions about what a little boy his age should or should not be doing that you accept him completely. He senses that and responds." Swearing under his breath, he pounded the seam of the top box with a fist. Without benefit of a knife, he slipped his fingers into the small slit he'd made and pulled the carton open.

"I'm sorry," she said, and meant it. "But I'm not sorry you had me here. You were right. I couldn't have gone home. I was too weak at the beginning."

She waited for him to pick up on the suggestion and ask how she was feeling now. Instead, he pulled books from the carton and stalked off toward a far shelf. Several minutes later, after he'd taken his time putting those books in the appropriate spots, he was back for more.

"I talked with Christine and Gideon today," she said lightly. "They agreed about postponing the open house. Chris was actually relieved, because some of the furniture for the model didn't come in right, and with the extra time, she can have it done over. She wants everything to be perfect." The last sentence was spoken more loudly to follow John down another aisle with another arm load of books.

Again he was several minutes arranging the books on the shelves. By the time he returned, Nina was growing uneasy.

"Aren't you going to talk to me?"

He was loading his arms a third time. "When you say something worthwhile. So far, all I've heard is babble." Off he went.

"It'd help if you'd stop working and look me in the eye," she called, growing annoyed. She waited until he returned before muttering, "And you tell me *I* work too much."

"These books have to be shelved." Tossing one empty carton aside, he started in on the second.

"Right now?"

"Is there something more worthwhile I should be doing?"

"Talking with me."

"Worthwhile, I said. There's nothing worthwhile in what we have to say to each other."

"There might be, if you could stop running back and forth with those books."

His answer to that was to head in a different direction with a new arm load.

"John! *Please!*" On impulse, she took right off after him, following him down a short aisle and around a corner. "I want to talk with you."

He was already putting one book after another in line. "What about?"

"You. How you've been. What you've been doing."

"Well," he said, raising the last six books and wedging them in a bunch onto the shelf, "I've been fine and doing all the same things I always do, so that'd be a pretty worthless conversation." He turned to leave.

"*John*," Nina cried, unable to take any more of his running. "*Don't!*"

Her cry must have reached him, because he stopped in his tracks. At first his body was straight. With an expelled breath, it seemed to sag a little. Cocking a hand on one lean hip, he hung his head and stood, silent, with his back to her.

She wanted to reach out and touch him, but didn't dare. Nor, though, could she let him go. More quietly, a little desperately, she said, "Talk with me. Just for a minute. Please?"

At first, she thought he'd refuse. When she was about to repeat her plea, even to intensify it, he straightened his spine and turned slowly. Spreading his arms along the bookshelf at shoulder height, he leaned back against the books and looked her in the eye.

"What did you want to say?"

She saw it then, saw hurt in his eyes, saw confusion and vulnerability and wanting. Long fingers clenched around her heart. She let out a small breath, then swallowed.

"I'm listening," he said evenly.

Swallowing again, she started toward him. Guilelessly, thinking only to tell him what she was feeling, she said, "I've missed you."

"You could have called to tell me that."

"I didn't know it until tonight."

"It just—" arms still outspread, he snapped his fingers "—came to you?"

"Seeing you." Stopping before him, she raised a hand to his face. "I've never missed anyone before." She brushed the wayward hair from his brow, but it fell right back in the way she loved. Entranced by that and by a tug she felt inside, she rasped a palm over the shadow of his beard, touched fingertips to his chin, then his mouth. Unable to help herself, she went up on tiptoe.

"Nina—"

"Don't move," she said in a hoarse whisper, and before he could say another word, she put her mouth to his. It was a simple touch at first, a sweet homecoming that was repeated with additional little touches and tastes. "I've missed you," she whispered again, going up this time for a deeper kiss. His lips resisted. She stroked them gently, traced them with the tip of her tongue, nipped at them until they began to soften. When he opened them enough to allow her entrance, she slipped her tongue inside. He tasted wonderful, so warm and exciting, so like John that when he began to respond to her kiss, she gave a totally helpless moan.

Startled by the sound, she dropped back to her heels. Watching her, John's eyes were alert. They seemed to question and warn, but she was beyond answering and heeding. The only thing she was capable of doing was touching him in response to a clamoring need inside. Raising trembling hands to his shoulders, she tested his strength there before moving inward to the buttons of his shirt.

"Nina, what—"

"Shh. Let me." One by one, she released the buttons, finally spreading the still-damp material to the sides. From the first time she'd seen him bare, she had known he was beautifully made, but memory paled before the real thing. Slightly awed, she caught her breath. Her hands skimmed lightly over his skin, over the cording of muscles higher up, over the wedge of hair that tapered toward his belly, over the dark, flat nipples that grew hard and tight. He was warm and gentle yet masculine through and through. Unable to deny herself the pleasure she leaned forward and put her mouth where her hands had been.

He whispered her name. She shushed him again, this time against the soft hair that swirled over the swells of his chest. She pressed her lips to one spot, put her tongue to another, dragged her teeth over a third. Only once did she stop, with her ear to the rapid thud of his heart and the pad of her thumb on his nipple, but if what she was doing excited him, it excited her as well. While her mouth continued its loving sport, her hands fell to the snap of his shorts.

Again he whispered her name, this time taking his arms from the shelves and framing her head. Still she hushed him. She kissed him lightly, one spot to the next on his chest, while she unzipped him and slipped her hands inside. He was hard and hot, a binding brand against her palm. She traced his length, curved her fingers around him and drew him up, then repeated the stroking until he began to shake.

"Oh, Nina, that feels good."

It was all she needed to hear. Working her way down from his breast, she kissed a trail over his navel to the thick nest of hair that flared at his groin. When she opened her mouth on the velvet tip of his sex, he tried to pull back.

"I'll come, baby, I'll come." His voice was a tortured moan, the sound of a man in the deepest stages of want.

The sound excited her beyond belief. Defying the hands that clenched and unclenched around her head, she loved him in ways she'd never loved a man before, and when his release came she stayed with him, showing him without words how much he meant to her.

Between harsh gasps, he whispered her name. His body seemed held erect by nothing more than the wild trembling that shook it. As the trembling eased, he slid down down until he was keeling, face-to-face with her. Hands in her hair, he looked at her for the longest time until, brokenly, he said, "No one's ever done that to me before."

"Then it was a first for us both," she whispered back.

His thumbs brushed her cheekbones, his lips caught hers. He drew her against him, only to ease her back in the next breath and tug her shirt from her shorts. "I need to feel you against me," he whispered as he unhooked her bra, and in the next instant he pushed her shorts to her knees and drew her in close again.

Nina couldn't contain the bubble of desire that swelled from her throat into a ragged moan. Large, capable hands covered her back, then her bottom, then worked their way to her breast and her belly.

"Does it hurt?" he asked by her ear, fingering the scar that was still too new to have faded.

Her breath was warm against his neck. "Once in a while, just a pinch."

"Can I make love to you?" he whispered.

"I wish you would," she whispered back.

Very gently then, with a care that brought tears to her eyes and small sighs of pleasure to her lips, he lowered her to the carpet, removed her shorts and his, and filled the place inside that had been wanting him so. Though he held his weight off her stomach, his penetration was deep. He let her set the pace, but he was attuned to her every need. When she grew hotter and her body began straining toward his, he used his fingers to help her to a stunning climax. His own followed soon after, leaving them in a limp tangle of arms and legs.

Snuggling closer into his embrace, Nina whispered a broken, "Oh, John, I was beginning to think you hated me."

He took a long, deep, shuddering breath. "Not hated. Loved. Love, present tense. I love you." Her fingers flew to his mouth, but the words were already out. Taking her wrist, he anchored her hand on his chest. "I do, Nina, and it's hell. I want to be with you all the time, but you have this thing for independence. I've been in agony all week, waiting for you to call."

Shaken by the depth of his feeling, by the intensity in the amber eyes that peered down at her, by the intensity of all *she* was feeling inside in the wake of his declaration, she managed a meek, "You could have called me."

"No. I insisted you come here from the hospital, and while you were here, I insisted you lie around and be coddled. I couldn't insist anymore. You wanted to fly. It was your turn to take the initiative."

She remembered words that had been spoken in anger and frustration on the day she'd left. "You said you were independent and self-sufficient, too."

"I am," he said quickly, then slowly to a more pensive pace, "but it's not how I want to live my life. I don't see anything weak about wanting a woman the way I want you. I don't see anything weak about wanting to sleep with a woman, or talk with her over breakfast and dinner, or take her to the beach, or eat the chocolate chip cookies she bakes. I don't see that I'd be losing anything by committing myself to you—" he took a deep breath, but when he went on, his voice was harder "—unless you don't make the same kind of commitment in return. I can't live the way I have been this week, Nina. I can't live in a vacuum, thinking of you, wondering, worrying, wanting. I can't sit around waiting for you to call when you chance to get a free minute. And I can't put J.J. through that."

Hearing his words, feeling the beat of his heart and the warm draw of his spent body, Nina was in heaven and hell at the same time. "What are you telling me?"

He was awhile in answering, and during that time, she had the awful feeling that he was savoring the last bits of pleasure before it all fell apart. She was feeling nervous when he finally took a deep breath and spoke.

"I'm saying," he began slowly and with conviction, "that I've been down this road before, only this time there's so much more of my heart involved that I can't, just can't take the risk. I love you, Nina, but if you don't love me back, if you can't marry me and move in here with me and cut back on your work so you can be a wife to me and a mother to J.J., I don't want it." He took another breath, a more labored one this time. "I guess maybe it is all or nothing. I can respect your work. I'd be the first to insist that you keep it up, and if you had an appointment at dinnertime once in a while, I certainly wouldn't complain. But work can't come first in your life. I have to. That's the only way it can be with me. I'm sorry."

Nina wanted to cry. Exerting the utmost control not to, she carefully pushed herself up. "Then—"

"Either we do it my way, or not at all," he said, rising to look her straight in the eye. "Either you love me, or you don't. Either we're together the way we should be, or we break it off. Cold turkey. Over. No phone calls. No visits. No 'maybe, if we find the time.'"

"But . . . that's not fair."

"Maybe not to you. You'd be just as happy to let things ride for years. But I can't do it. I feel too much."

She was incredulous. "You love me so much you'd give me up in a minute? That doesn't make any sense, John!"

The only response he made was a slow shrug.

"John," she pleaded. When he didn't answer but simply sat there staring at her, she was suddenly lashed by conflicting emotions. She wanted to rant and rave, to hit him, to knock some sense into him; at the same time, she wanted to throw herself into his arms and beg him to hold her, to love her, to keep on loving her while she did what she had to in life.

Overwhelmed and confused, she did the only practical thing she could at that moment. She reached for her shorts and pulled them on to cover her nakedness that had felt so right such a short time before.

"You're leaving then?" he asked.

"I have to. I can't think. I feel confused. I don't know what to do. I need time."

"I don't have time, Nina," he said in a grim voice. "The longer this goes on, the more it hurts."

"Loving shouldn't hurt."

"But it does."

She knew she should argue or plead or throw herself at him and make love to him again and again, until she was so firmly entrenched under his skin that he wouldn't be able to shake her no matter how hard he tried.

But she had too much dignity for that. Pushing her feet into her sneakers, concentrating on willing away the tears that seemed bent on pooling in her lids, fighting the odd sense of near-panic gripping her insides, she stood, straightened her T-shirt and started walking toward the door.

One word from John and she would have stopped. But that word didn't come, so she continued on out into the warm summer night and drove home, shivering all the way.

10

NINA WENT TO WORK the next morning, but her heart wasn't in it. She hadn't slept well and was feeling tired and sore and, in general, disinterested in anything to do with real estate. When, after four hours of moving in and out of the office with and without clients, she'd had enough, she prevailed on an accommodating Lee to take over the few appointments she'd made for the afternoon.

Back in her apartment, she was at loose ends. There wasn't anything she wanted to do there, and though she was tired, she couldn't sleep. No sooner did she close her eyes than images appeared behind her lids that kept her awake—John standing on the beach looking out to sea, or kneeling by the tub bathing J.J., or lying naked from the waist down on The Leaf Turner's carpet, between the shelves for Self-Help and Romance. Each image brought back a memory in vivid detail. Each one haunted her.

The one image that kept returning, though, the one that haunted her the most, was the scene in J.J.'s bedroom. She was on the bed with J.J. tucked up against her. A large book was open on their laps, but their eyes were on John, who was telling the story with his hands.

Over and over Nina saw that scene, each time struck by something different. Once there was the warmth—maternal, if she dared use that word to describe what she felt—of holding J.J. in her arms. Another time there was the magnitude of her feeling for John, the sense of trust and respect and attraction that she'd never felt for any other man. Yet another time—and repeatedly— there was the totally unexpected contentment of being a part of an intimate family scene.

John had said that loving her hurt. In those long hours at home, she came to feel the hurt herself. He had given her a glimpse of something she had never expected to experience, and where once ignorance had been bliss, she was ignorant no more. She knew the pain of tasting something exquisitely sweet.

But wasn't independence sweet? Wasn't self-sufficiency? Wasn't freedom?

The more questions she asked herself, the more confused and unhappy she grew. Friday night passed on leaden hands creeping around the clock. By the time Saturday morning arrived, she was feeling no more like going to work than she had the day before, and that unsettled her all the more. She loved her work, at least, she always had. Now, somehow, it seemed inconsequential.

What she wanted to do was to see John, but she couldn't.

Nor could she call a friend. Or take a drive. Or go to the beach. Or the supermarket. Or a movie. She couldn't do anything frivolous, not when she was confronting the most momentous decision she'd ever had to make in her life.

What she did, acting on an instinct that was so nearly subconscious that she couldn't possibly give it much thought, was to pick up the phone and call first the airport, then Lee, then pack a small bag and head for Omaha.

WITHIN MINUTES of her arrival at the nursing home where her mother lived, Anthony Kimball strode out to greet her. "I'm glad you're here, Nina," he said. After shaking the hand she offered, he guided her down the hall. "I wasn't sure you'd gotten my message. When you didn't return the call—"

"What call?"

"The one I made this morning." He frowned. "You didn't get the message?"

"No." She felt the rise of a cold fear inside. "Is she worse?"

He nodded. With quiet compassion, he said, "It won't be long now. It's good that you've come." At her mother's room, he opened the door. With a sense of dread, Nina stepped inside and moved toward the bed. The tiny figure that lay there seemed little more than a skeleton under a token blanket of skin.

Nina was horrified. "She's so thin."

"The last few months have been hard for her."

"But she doesn't know that," Nina said a bit frantically.

"No."

The reassurance was welcome but brief. The very same instinct that had put Nina on the plane that morning was telling her that, as the doctor had said, her mother's death was at hand. And though she had never been close to Maria Stone, though Maria had let her down again and again, though there had been times when Nina had actually hated her, blood was thicker than water. Maria, for all her weaknesses, was still her mother.

Nina didn't realize that the mournful sound she heard came from her own throat until the doctor touched her shoulder. "If you'd rather wait in my office—"

"No," she said and, though determined, her voice was thin, "I want to stay here with her."

She did just that. Sitting in the chair that the doctor brought to the side of the bed, she held her mother's frail hand, studied her expressionless face, stroked her thin gray hair and pretended that things had been different.

Hours passed, still she stayed in that chair. After a time, though, she stopped pretending, because memories started coming from nowhere at all, memories that she hadn't known she had for events she hadn't known she'd lived through. She remembered being very little, falling off a curb and skinning her knees, then being held by a woman with the same delicate profile as this woman on the bed. She remembered fishing funny little noodles out of a soup that she loved, while the woman who had made that soup, a woman with the same bow-shaped mouth as this woman on the bed, looked on and laughed. She remembered the sound of that laugh, and the smell of perfume. She remembered the way that smell had clung to her after she'd been hugged tightly by a woman with slender, fine-shaped hands that, in a healthier time, could well have been those of this woman on the bed.

There had been good times, she realized with a start. There had been some smiles between the frowns, only she'd been so overwhelmed by the need to survive in those frightening times that she'd forgotten them. They had been lost, probably would have been lost forever, had she not, through the force of fate, taken the time out to spend these last hours with her mother.

She wondered at the solace she might have had over the years if she'd taken that time sooner. She wondered whether she would have felt less anger toward Maria and less pity for herself. She wondered whether she might have been more complete a woman. For so long, she had believed that she'd risen way above anything her mother had been. Suddenly she wasn't so sure. Her mother had given her life, then in her own way and working around her own limitations, had loved her. Nina hadn't given anyone life or love. She had been too wrapped up in her own drive to prove that she didn't need either.

But she'd been wrong. Sitting there by her mother's bedside, holding tightly to the hand that had long ago held hers, Nina understood things about herself that she would never have considered before. As the hours wore on, as Maria's skin grew more waxy and her breathing more shallow, Nina was humbled.

Anthony Kimball stopped in before he left for the day. Nurses checked in and out, monitoring Maria's state at the same time that they offered Nina hot coffee and snacks, most of which she refused. She felt a great emptiness inside, an emptiness that wasn't totally foreign to her, but she wasn't hungry. All she wanted to do was to sit by her mother's side, to talk softly on the chance that she could be heard, to warm Maria's cold hands, to let her presence be felt.

She never knew if it was. Shortly after dawn the next morning, when the sun rose with a joy Nina didn't feel, Maria took a last breath and slipped away.

NINA HAD HER BURIED later that afternoon under a pretty dogwood in a small cemetery on the outskirts of town. After thanking the priest for his kind words and Anthony Kimball for his kind care, she took a cab to the airport. From there, just as her flight was being called, she phoned John.

As though he'd been waiting, he picked up after the very first ring. "Hello?"

With a fast indrawn breath, she said a timid, "John?"

His voice softened. "Nina. Ah, Nina, thank goodness you've called. I've been so worried. Are you in Omaha?"

She nodded, then realized he couldn't see, and said a small, "Uh-huh."

"How is she?"

"Gone. Early this morning—" Her voice cracked. She pressed a hand to her mouth.

"Oh, God, baby, I'm sorry."

"Maybe—" she cleared her throat of the tightness there "—maybe it's for the best."

"Maybe," he said quietly.

"But it's hard—" Again her voice cracked.

"Are you all right?" he asked very softly.

"Uh, I think so." She gulped in a breath. "John?"

"Yes?"

"I'm coming home now. I want—I need—you. Can you—"

"What time? What flight?"

She gave him the information, then hung up the phone and, brushing the tears from her eyes, boarded the plane. She didn't cry during the flight. Nor did she eat or sleep. She felt in a state of suspended emotion, too tired to think or feel, but waiting, holding herself together as best she could.

The plane was fifteen minutes late in landing, which was late indeed, given that it was due in well after eleven Boston time. Putting the strap of her overnight case on her shoulder, Nina followed the rest of the passengers down the aisle of the plane. Passing through the jetway, her throat began to tighten. By the time she made it into the terminal, her eyes were filling up again. Her step slowed as she looked around. She swallowed. She said a silent prayer.

Then she saw John. He was standing off to the side, out of the path of the passengers. Wearing his glasses and a somber expression, he looked tense.

Slowly she started toward him. Her heart was in her mouth, ahead of every other one of the emotions that were clogging her throat, but she kept her feet moving, kept her composure intact. Only when she stood directly before him, when she could feel the warmth, the strength and caring that were hers for the taking, did everything she'd been keeping inside swell up and spill over. Wordlessly she slipped her arms around his waist, buried her face against his throat and began to cry.

At what point his arms closed around her she didn't know, though she felt his support from the start. She cried softly but steadily, unable to stem the tears, barely trying. She cried for her mother, for the years and the love that had been lost, and when she was done crying for those things, she cried for all she'd put John through.

His collar was damp from her tears by the time her sobs slowed, and by then, the strain of the past thirty-six hours was taking its toll. Bone weary, she mustered scattered bits of strength to raise her eyes to his and utter a whispered plea. "Take me home?"

Something in her tear-damp eyes must have elaborated on the request, because, without a word, John slipped an arm around her waist and helped her out the door to the car. Once inside, he brought her close to his side. Then he drove straight to the small white Victoria that he called home, led her upstairs and, with the most heartrendingly gentle kiss, put her to bed.

THE SKY WAS NEWLY PINK in the east when Nina opened her eyes again. Though her memory of the night before was vague, she knew instantly that she was in John's home, in John's bed, wearing another one of John's large shirts. John wasn't as decently dressed. Bare to the hip, at which point he disappeared under the sheet, he was propped on an elbow, watching her. His expression didn't give away anything of what he was thinking.

The lack of knowing, the fear that brought, dashed all remnants of sleep. With a nervous half smile, she said, "Hi."

"How are you feeling?" he returned without any kind of smile.

She was quiet for a minute, looking into his eyes, wanting to melt into him but knowing it was time to talk. So she said, "Sad. Happy. Scared."

"That's a lot. Want to run through them for me one by one?"

Thinking about what she wanted to say was difficult. For a minute, her throat knotted and she thought she might cry again. Determined to be stronger than that, she forced the words out. "Sad, because she's gone and I never really knew her. Happy, because being with her Saturday taught me something that I might not have otherwise known. Scared, because I know where I want to go now, but I'm not sure I'm worthy of it." Her voice broke, still she went on. "I've been blind about lots of things."

"Like what?" he asked, his eyes level.

"Like her, and the fact that she loved me, even though she was so screwed up she couldn't show it much of the time.

"That happens to lots of parents."

"I know. But I didn't know it when I was growing up, so I got bitter and angry and blamed her for everything that was missing in my life." Her voice dropped. "But I was the one responsible for lots of those things being missing."

"What things?"

"A home and family. Close relationships. I set out to become independently rich, which was something my mother had never been. I was sure that would be a panacea, and I wasn't letting anyone or anything get in my way. Work would fill up my life, I thought. I thought being busy and successful would be enough. But it isn't."

"How do you know?"

"Because," she searched helplessly for the words, "it just isn't."

"Why not?"

"Because—" she wished she could say what she was feeling, but the emotions were so strong, so momentous, so frightening "—it's not the same."

"The same as what?"

"*Being* with people."

"Being?"

"Living with people."

"As in cohabitating?"

"*Loving* people."

John was very still. His amber eyes grew darker, more alert than before. "Are you in love?" he asked softly.

Eyes large and locked with his, she nodded.

"With me?"

Again she nodded.

For the first time, she saw a softening of his expression. "For a lady who can talk up a storm when she wants to make a sale, you're sure having trouble with this."

"That's because it's so important."

"Is it?"

She nodded. "More important than anything I've ever said or done before in my life."

"So. Tell me what you're thinking. Just spit it out."

Taking courage from the gentleness of his face, she said, "I'm thinking that I don't want to be like that lady you once described. I don't want to wake up one day and be alone and empty and too old to have kids." She took a tremulous breath. "I'm thinking that I love you, and want to live here with you and be a mother to J.J. and maybe be a mother to kids we could have. I mean," she hurried to add, "I don't know anything about changing a diaper or making a bottle, but I could learn, if you wanted more kids. But you may not. J.J. is special, and he takes twice as much love."

"I've got more than that," John said softly. Cupping a hand to her face, he rubbed his thumb over her lips. "I've got more than enough for you and him and a bunch of others."

"I want a bunch. That's what I want."

"What about work?"

"I'll work. Just not all the time."

John looked skeptical. "Will that be possible?"

"You were the one who said it was."

"But is it for you? You love your work. It's been your life for so long—"

"Until I met you. It hasn't been the same since. Nothing's been the same since."

He grinned then, the grin she found so sexy, the one that could make her insides go all hot and soft. "I like the sound of that. Now, if I could just hear those other little words again."

She knew which ones he wanted. Swallowing down the last of her fears, she said, "I love you."

"Again."

They came more easily this time. "I love you."

"One more time."

She grinned. It was a snap. "I love you."

Shifting under the sheets, John rolled over so that his long body fit hers. Linking their fingers on either side of her head, he effected a slow undulation of his hips. "Now if we could have the words with a little kiss, then a little touch, then a little—" A loud sound in the hall cut him off. "Damn," he muttered, rolled off Nina and yanked the sheet up to cover her completely. "J.J.'s up."

"He's saying 'daddy'?" she whispered from under the sheet. Her hand was on his hip. She left it there.

"Yup." The door opened and his voice picked up. "Hi, sport, how're you doing?" From under the sheet, Nina could feel the movement as he signed. Seconds later, she felt a small bundle hit the end of the bed, but it slid off nearly as quickly, followed by the patter of small feet leaving the room on the run. "Smart kid," John muttered. "He saw your clothes. He's off to the guest room." Leaning close to the sheet, he warned, "Last chance, Nina. If he finds you in my bed, there's no going back. I can still make up some excuse for your clothes—"

Her hand slid over his hip just far enough to make him jump. "What excuse will you give for this?" He was still fully aroused.

"Uh, he doesn't have to, uh, see that. Damn it, Nina, don't play with me now. Are you staying, or aren't you? I have to know for sure."

"For J.J.?"

"For *me*. He'll have his own life, and I want mine. I want you in it. What do you say?"

"I may be a lousy wife."

"I'll take that chance."

"I may be a lousy mother."

"No way. Come on, Nina. Is it a yes?"

Beneath the sheets, Nina was flying high as a kite. "I need the magic words."

"I love you."

"Again."

"I love you!"

"Louder."

"*I love you!*"

The shout was barely out when the patter of feet announced J.J.'s return. "Didn't find her?" Nina heard John ask. She felt movement, then all was suspiciously quiet until, with a gleeful guffaw, J.J. pulled back the sheet and jumped on the bed. John caught him seconds before he would have pounced on Nina's stomach, but she was up and laughing, being hugged by them both in no time flat.

Never before had she felt so happy, so whole, so loved.

Epilogue

THE SUN WAS WARM on their skin, but it felt good. The winter had been a long, snowy one. Spring had finally come.

Leaning back against John, whose body was a more comfortable chaise than any other she had ever tried, Nina took a deep, deep breath and let it out in an appreciative, "Mmm, does this feel good?"

His mouth tickled her ear. "The sun or me?"

She hooked her arms around his thighs, which rose alongside her hips. "Both. This is an absolutely gorgeous spot."

They were at Crosslyn Rise, sprawled on the lawn that sloped toward the sea. Behind them, on the crest of the hill, stood the mansion, its multichimneyed roof, newly pointed bricks and bright white Georgian columns setting it off against a backdrop of evergreen lushness and azure sky. To the left and right were more trees, many newly budded, and beyond the trees, grouped in clusters, were two dozen condominiums, all finished, all occupied, all spectacular. Before them, at the foot of the hill, was the small marina with its pristine docks and proud-masted yachts, and the row of shops that included an art gallery, a clothing boutique, a sports shop, a video store, two small restaurants, a drugstore and The Leaf Turner.

"Are you sorry we didn't buy a place here?" John asked.

"Not on your life. It's enough that you have the bookstore. Besides, I love the Victorian, especially now." As soon as John had moved the Leaf Turner to Crosslyn Rise, they had repossessed the first floor of the house. What with the professional expertise of Carter Molloy and Gideon and Christine Lowe, they had renovated the place into something neither one of them had dared dream of. Nina might have done even more—finished the attic as a playroom for J.J. or built on an attached garage—had not John been vehement that the bulk of her Crosslyn Rise profit was to go into an account in her own name. He didn't care if it sat there untouched for years, he told her, just so long as she knew it was there, for her, should she want or need it.

He understood where she'd come from. He was special that way.

But then, she mused, lazily shifting her bare feet in the warm, soft grass, he was special in lots of ways. Like his concern for her. There was times when she could swear that his only goal in life was to make her happy.

"Are you sure," his deep voice came now, "that you wouldn't like to rent a small space here for you?"

"Can't do," she said with pride. "We're leased to one-hundred-percent capacity."

"But when something opens up."

"Nope. I'm happy where I am." She was still at Crown Realty, with Chrissie handling her pink slips and Lee, albeit engaged to a wonderful guy now, backing her up.

"You don't ever think about having your own agency, not even for a minute, for old times' sake?"

Tipping her head against his arm, she looked up into his face. How many times she'd seen those strong features in the past two years, seen them in every light and mood, and it seemed that she only loved each one more. "When do I have time to think about having my own agency? My life is so full." Full as opposed to busy. There was a difference.

"But you wanted to be independent."

"I am. I work when I want and come home when I want." She touched his cheek. "It's a pretty nice deal." She paused. "Why don't you look convinced?"

"I just worry sometimes. I think back to when I met you and remember all the things you wanted—"

"What did I want?" she cut in to ask in a rhetorical way. "I wanted my own business, but that doesn't mean anything to me now, because I have enough else to do that I don't want the responsibility. I wanted lots of money, and I have it, right in the bank."

"You wanted freedom—"

"Which is just what I've got. You've made me free." The words had slipped out on their own, but she thought about them for a minute, finally saying a soft and knowing, "It's true. I used to think that loving meant being a slave to another human being. But loving you isn't that way at all. You make me feel whole and important and secure. You give me strength to do new things." With a mischievous grin, she said, "I've bloomed."

Chuckling, he moved his hand over the flaming orange tunic that covered her belly. "Just a little, but it's in there."

Covering his hand, she held it fast where it was as she looked up into his eyes. "I'm so excited," she whispered, barely able to contain it.

"Not scared?"

"Sure, scared."

"But you've been a super mom to J.J."

"J.J.'s a big boy." Her eyes took on an added glow. "He's doing so well. I'm so proud of him." The special school he was at—the one John had financed with his share of the profit from Crosslyn Rise—was doing wonderful things for him. He had lots of friends. He was reading, writing, signing, lipreading, even talking in his way. He, too, was blooming. "But a little baby, a little baby is different."

"We'll do it together," John said with quiet confidence.

Doing things together was pretty much the story of their marriage, which was another reason why Nina hadn't once felt that she'd given something up in teaming with John. He was an able man, an able father and husband. He had been just as self-sufficient, as she before they'd met, and he could easily be self-sufficient, as could she. The fact that they chose to share whatever load it was they were bearing at a given time, was a tribute to their mutual respect and love.

In the months since they had been married, Nina had done something she had sworn never to do. She had grown dependent—dependent on John for his love. But while once that would have terrified her, it didn't now. She trusted him. She knew beyond a shadow of a doubt that she would always have his love.

Feeling happy and hopeful, if hopelessly smitten with the man holding her, Nina gazed out over the picturesque scene ahead and sighed in utter contentment. "There's something about this place. Carter said it once, and I think it's true. There's something in the air here. Crosslyn Rise is a charm. Look at Carter and Jessica and how happy they are with that beautiful little girl of theirs." She grinned. "I'm glad they bought the unit in the meadow. It's perfect for them."

John kissed the top of her head, then murmured into her hair, "It seems right to have a Crosslyn still here."

"Mmm. Even though they spend weeks at a time with Carter's folks in Florida. I understand it's a fantastic place that Carter bought for them." She took a quick breath. "And speaking of fantastic places, the one Gideon is building in Lincoln is going to be *incredible*—" savvy broker that she was, she couldn't resist tacking on a self-righteous "—even if he did overpay for the land."

"He has the money. Crosslyn Rise did well for him."

"In many respects—money, reputation, love. They're so happy, he and Chris. I love seeing them together."

John flashed his wristwatch in front of her nose. "Is it time?"

She shook her head against his chest. "We have another five minutes." Since the Crosslyn Rise consortium had formally disbanded, the three couples—the Malloys, the Lowes and the Sawyers—had taken to getting together once a month or so. Sometimes it was for dinner, sometimes for a show, sometimes for an evening of general playing at one or another of their homes. On this particular day, they were having an impromptu lunch at one of the small restaurants on the pier. Nina was looking forward to it.

Even more, though, she was looking forward to spending the rest of the day with John. Though he was working full-time in the store now that J.J. was in school, he had arranged to have Minna Larken cover for him that afternoon. Likewise, Nina had scheduled all of her appointments for the morning. So they were free. Nina had her monthly checkup with the doctor, which John refused to miss, but after that they were heading into Boston for several hours of walking and shopping and sipping cappucino in sidewalk cafés. They would pick J.J. up at school on the way home.

It was a wonderful life, Nina mused, and all because of John. Shifting impulsively to face him, she slipped one arm around his neck. "Do you know how much I love you, John Sawyer?"

The question alone was enough to bring pleasure to his face, which, in turn, enhanced hers. "I think so," he answered with a soft half smile, "but I wouldn't mind if you told me again."

She didn't have to. Slipping her other arm around his neck, she gave him a long, breath-robbing, arm-throbbing hug that said it all.

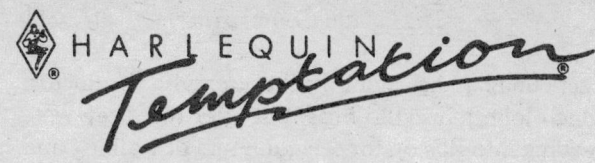

From the author of
DADDY, DARLING

DOCTOR, DARLING
by
Glenda Sanders

The eagerly awaited sequel to DADDY, DARLING is here! In DOCTOR, DARLING, the imposing Dr. Sergei Karol meets his match. He's head over heels in love with Polly Mechler, the adorable TV celebrity whose plumbing-supply commercials have made her a household name. But Sergei wants Polly to be adorable just for him . . . and Polly isn't one to follow doctor's orders!

Watch for DOCTOR, DARLING.
Coming in January 1991

TDDR

Harlequin romances are now available in stores at these convenient times each month.

Harlequin Presents **Harlequin American Romance** **Harlequin Historical** **Harlequin Intrigue**	These series will be in stores on the 4th of every month.
Harlequin Romance **Harlequin Temptation** **Harlequin Superromance** **Harlequin Regency Romance**	New titles for these series will be in stores on the 16th of every month.

We hope this new schedule is convenient for you. With only two trips each month to your local bookseller, you will always be sure not to miss any of your favorite authors!

Happy reading!

Please note there may be slight variations in on-sale dates in your area due to differences in shipping and handling.

Take 4 bestselling love stories FREE
Plus get a FREE surprise gift!

He drove her to distraction

Nina Stone was a go-getter. As the broker for the Crosslyn Rise development—and an investor—she was on the fast track to success. But John Sawyer and his infernal dawdling were holding her back.

John also had a stake in the Rise, but he was in no hurry to approve her sales plan. *He* had a life outside of this deal—his son, his bookstore . . . his growing attraction for the passionate, driven Nina Stone. And John was about to prove to Nina that slow and steady *definitely* had its merits. . . .

ISBN 0-373-25425-3

25425

0 65373 00275 4

PRINTED IN U.S.A.